PENGU

edwin + matilda

Laurence Fearnley is the author of six novels. Her second novel, *Room*, was shortlisted for the Montana New Zealand Book Awards in 2001. She has been awarded several fellowships, notably the 2004 Artists to Antarctica fellowship, the 2006 Island of Residencies fellowship in Tasmania, and the 2007 Robert Burns fellowship at the University of Otago.

Based in Dunedin, she is currently working on the third book in her southern trilogy.

edwin + matilda

Laurence Fearnley

PENGUIN BOOKS

PENGUIN BOOKS
Published by the Penguin Group
Penguin Group (NZ), 67 Apollo Drive, Rosedale,
North Shore 0632, New Zealand (a division of Pearson New Zealand Ltd)
Penguin Group (USA) Inc., 375 Hudson Street,
New York, New York 10014, USA
Penguin Group (Canada), 90 Eglinton Avenue East, Suite 700, Toronto,
Ontario, M4P 2Y3, Canada (a division of Pearson Penguin Canada Inc.)
Penguin Books Ltd, 80 Strand, London, WC2R 0RL, England
Penguin Ireland, 25 St Stephen's Green,
Dublin 2, Ireland (a division of Penguin Books Ltd)
Penguin Group (Australia), 250 Camberwell Road, Camberwell,
Victoria 3124, Australia (a division of Pearson Australia Group Pty Ltd)
Penguin Books India Pvt Ltd, 11, Community Centre,
Panchsheel Park, New Delhi – 110 017, India
Penguin Books (South Africa) (Pty) Ltd, 24 Sturdee Avenue,
Rosebank, Johannesburg 2196, South Africa
Penguin Books Ltd, Registered Offices: 80 Strand, London, WC2R 0RL, England

First published by Penguin Group (NZ), 2007
1 3 5 7 9 10 8 6 4 2

Designed by Vivianne Douglas
Typeset by Egan Reid
Printed in Australia by McPherson's Printing Group

ISBN 978 014 300739 5

A catalogue record for this book is available
from the National Library of New Zealand.
www.penguin.co.nz

ARTS COUNCIL OF NEW ZEALAND *Toi Aotearoa*

The assistance of Creative New Zealand towards the production of this book
is gratefully acknowledged by the Publisher.

For Garry and Sue, with love

Even though it began when I kissed Edwin, I remember lying awake and thinking, Matilda, what on earth are you doing? For a moment I felt overtaken by panic: here I was in bed with a man who was older than almost anyone I knew, older than anyone I had ever been close to – and we had just made love. I recalled thinking, I've got to get out of here. This is nuts. But I didn't move. Instead, like a naturalist observing a rare or endangered species, I lay very still and watched. And I waited to see what would happen.

I had spent much of the day watching him. I hadn't been able to think of too much to say – I was so tired – but I liked looking at him. I thought he was handsome. I liked the clothes he wore: faded brown corduroy trousers that were a fraction too long for his height – they were frayed a little around the hem from where they scuffed against the ground. He seemed to have two jerseys: one navy blue, the other a rich chocolate brown. They were both nice and I got the impression, looking at them, that he probably washed them by hand. They weren't in the least bit felted – unlike my jumpers. They were soft and they suited him.

I'd assumed, when I'd first seen him, that he was a tall man but later it dawned on me that he was less than six foot – maybe five foot eight or nine. When he walked he was graceful, and – this is odd – I imagined walking next to him. To see myself walking beside him gave me pleasure. Why is that? I never saw him stumble, not once.

Best of all were his eyes: they were the kind of blue you see in faded flowers, once the intensity of the colour has been bleached by the sun. Borage, cornflower, thyme – any of those flowers that grow wild on the roadside. Roadside wildflower eyes – not shop-bought!

I liked the look of concentration on his face when we made love. His hands moved gently over my body; it was as if he was turning the pages of some fragile book – the type of book that has tissue pages, like an old-fashioned Bible. He reminded me, too, of a child learning to read. I pictured his fingertips tracing the words on the page, his lips mouthing the sounds, so intense was his focus. 'Edwin,' I teased, 'am I a good book?'

He didn't understand. An expression of confusion followed quickly by wonder crossed his face and it made me feel so happy. I even forgot that there was something wrong with me and I loved him for allowing me to forget.

I liked the contrasts of his body. Even though he was lean, there was a hint of softness around his stomach and waist. Across his chest grew short, wiry hairs and it gave me pleasure to ease my fingers through them. There is no way to describe the sensation except to say that I was reminded of walking barefoot across newly mown grass – in summer. Touching his body put me in mind of summer – and warmth.

I remember the first time I saw him naked. I got a shock, to tell the truth. I don't know what I'd been expecting but I was taken aback by the size of his penis. It was pretty large; I suppose subconsciously I had been expecting to see an old man's penis: something a little bit shrivelled or droopy or well worn – if there is such a thing. That was odd – the first time I saw his erect penis. It was so normal looking, despite the tufts of grey hair surrounding it.

Being in bed with Edwin made me think about a lot of things. I thought about how he was sixty-two, and instead of being in bed with a woman he had known a long time, someone with whom he had shared a lifetime's worth of experiences – marriage, children, career, family – he was with me. A woman he knew almost nothing about. And then I thought about me and how a woman of my age ought to be able to look ahead and plan a future with the man next to her. Yet that is something I can't allow myself to do. I don't want to think about the future – it's too lonely. Edwin and I have no past to remember and little future to look forward to. We are together now and that's enough.

I had wanted to sleep with him – and I don't think he slept with me just because he felt he had to, out of politeness. I hope not. I wouldn't want to spend the rest of my life with someone who just felt sorry for me.

I loved being with him and I didn't ever want to move. I wanted to stay next to him. As close and still as possible.

PART ONE

edwin

ONE

'My chick's better looking than yours!'

The voice broke Edwin's concentration. Looking up from his camera, he turned his attention away from the wedding couple framed in his viewfinder towards the sound behind him. He took in the faces of three youths sitting on the bonnet of a late-model Subaru. Dressed identically in brick-red shirts, grey waistcoats and grey trousers, they appeared to be in their twenties, local boys decked out as a wedding party. The one who called out was presumably the groom. From their slightly dishevelled appearance, Edwin guessed they had spent most of the afternoon inside the winery's tasting room. They'd probably had their photos taken earlier in the day – a day or two before the actual wedding, as was the trend these days – standing among the grapevines, vines so golden they seemed to capture the glow of the sun and reflect it back. It was a beautiful location, thought Edwin; no wonder it was such a popular choice with wedding parties.

His own groups had also come out to the vineyard a day before the ceremony. They would get their wedding photographs taken and then relax for a few hours: wandering along the vast rows of vines or simply sitting by the fireplace inside, tasting wine. In the old days couples booked the photographer just for the day itself, but these days there seemed to be no end to the number of times the bride and groom would don their outfits and pose for the camera. He was often booked for two sessions for each wedding, which cost the couple a great deal of money and increased the planning and stress.

The couple who had hired him this time, however, were playing it differently. They had booked him to take formal pictures prior to the wedding, but were going to record the actual ceremony themselves – with disposable cameras handed out to the guests on arrival. Edwin didn't mind: it was his last job before retiring and he no longer needed the work. Besides, it was their day; they were entitled to do whatever they wanted.

He took a deep breath and looked about him. Of all the vineyards in the area, this one, nestled in the hills behind Bannockburn, was his favourite. It had a view of not only the Clutha River in the distance but of the Kawarau, too. He loved the Kawarau. It was so blue it reminded him of the 'German poison' he used to make as a child: a drop of his father's ink added to a test-tube of water. The son of the medical superintendent, he had grown up in a tuberculosis sanatorium perched on the hill above Waipiata in the Maniototo. It was still there, the sanatorium – his home. Surrounded by ex-servicemen returned from the war, he had created a fantasy world for himself – one in which he single-handedly poisoned the Germans and saved Waipiata from Japanese invasion.

Glancing now at the rows of poplar trees before him he felt light-headed. In a few more days he would be free. After so many years of being tied to a small business, it seemed impossible.

He turned back to the couple in front of him. They seemed pleasant, though he had only dealt with Jacob, the groom. The bride appeared to have left the organisation of the photography to him, and she had been oddly quiet, almost watchful, all afternoon. The effect, Edwin found, was disconcerting. It struck him that she wasn't so much a participant as a spectator – and a vaguely detached one at that. Perhaps she was simply nervous – or tired, he concluded. In his experience, many brides were shattered by the time of the actual wedding. They had reached the point of being worn out and they simply wanted the photographs over and done with. It was one more chore to tick off, one more battle that needed to be faced.

The groom, although dressed in a respectable dark suit, reminded Edwin of one of those young men you saw on screen entering a courtroom. He appeared both uncomfortable and defiant, as if he was conscious of the fact that his suit was ill-fitting but had nevertheless persuaded himself not to show that he cared. There was something vaguely ludicrous about the groom's appearance: Edwin would have to work hard to draw attention away from the boy's 'look' in his photographs.

The girl was more difficult to read. Edwin focused on her now as he requested the couple to shuffle forward a few steps. She had an old-fashioned name – Matilda – and yet she looked young, very young, he thought – no more than eighteen or nineteen. Like the groom, she also looked uncomfortable, but rather than obscuring her discomfort with defiance, she had the appearance of someone who had grown used to it, as if discomfort was what defined her life and she had come to terms with it. She kept tugging at her gown, adjusting the thin straps of her dress which, unusually for a wedding gown, was a plain dark, midnight blue

– a colour that accentuated her almond-shaped eyes. She was small, slight, no more than five foot tall and reed-thin. Too thin, concluded Edwin. His thoughts drifted back to the sanatorium and the young women who arrived each week: skeletal patients, moon faces atop stick bodies, flesh wasting away as they sought his father's cure: fresh air and bed rest.

Matilda's hair was cut very short, as if it had recently been shaved and was just beginning to grow back. Yet it suited her. There was an aura of intensity about her, Edwin thought. It was strange to be confronted by a bride who looked so serious; one who stared back at him as if the camera was no more than a telescope. He had the impression that she could look through the camera and into his eyes and, although he knew it wasn't possible, he felt vulnerable.

In his experience, it was very rare for a subject to make eye contact with the photographer. It was even more unusual for a woman to do so. In most cases, women were too uncomfortable with – and critical of – their bodies to look through the camera at him. Only professional models had learnt how to face the camera. Other women held back, conscious of their supposed shortcomings. He was always amazed at the way women dissected themselves into parts rather than viewing themselves as complete: their ears were too prominent, their lips uneven, the skin around their eyes too puffy, their skin tone too red or blotchy, their hips too thin or too curvy. Even brides – women who had given hours of thought to make-up, hair and gowns – usually wore an expression of resignation. It was as if they knew the photograph would depict them not as they felt or wished to appear but as they really looked. For some reason, his subjects allowed themselves to believe that an image that took one-sixtieth of a second to make could be a truthful judge of character. As if a photograph could convey an entire life. In its purest form, it always came down to one question: am I beautiful?

Matilda, however, lacked the self-consciousness of other brides. Most, after all, felt obliged to smile – no matter what the circumstances of their union. But Matilda seemed oblivious to convention. Her mouth curled neither up nor down; it simply cut a straight line across her face, and it was that more than anything else that caught Edwin's attention. Her stitch mouth – that was what he focused on.

Although he had never put his theory to the test, Edwin felt that he could predict which marriages would be happy and which would fail from the way the wedding couples faced the camera. He'd happened to mention this once to his GP, Dr Aubrey, a man older than himself but someone he counted as a friend despite their never meeting socially. Dr Aubrey said he knew exactly what Edwin was talking about; indeed, he had often been struck by a similar sensation when delivering babies. That was in the old days, he'd emphasised, when doctors still carried out that type of service. He had drifted off for a few seconds, caught by a memory of his life as a young doctor, before pulling himself back to the present. Once in a while, he said, he would catch sight of a particular kind of anxious expression on a newborn's face that would cause him to hesitate and all but proclaim, 'Eh 'up, this one's in trouble.'

Edwin had nodded and asked, 'What happened to them? The anxious newborns?' to which Dr Aubrey responded that he'd only see them infrequently, that they'd been the children with ear infections, scabies or conjunctivitis. 'Sad little mites,' he'd murmured, looking up at Edwin.

'Were they all unhappy?' asked Edwin, warming to the subject. 'Good heavens no,' said Dr Aubrey. 'I'm sure there must have been some – perhaps among those I rarely saw – who lived long and happy lives. Though there was one . . .' he continued as an afterthought, 'who was killed in a riding incident. A seven-year-old. I wrote his death certificate.'

'Oh,' mumbled Edwin, surprised that he should experience any sense of loss for someone he had never known. 'Poor child.' Dr Aubrey had nodded and returned to the task of taking Edwin's blood pressure. And although the doctor said nothing more on the subject he couldn't help but nod, as if concluding that Edwin was almost certainly one of those children: a lonely, troubled child.

Edwin's thoughts were still on the doctor when the boy who had earlier called out, 'My chick's better looking than yours' suddenly shouted to Jacob, 'Don't do it, mate – do yourself a favour and find yourself a sex goddess, a girl like mine!' Despite himself, Edwin immediately turned around to see who he was talking about. He took in a tall young woman walking across the carpark towards the youths. Her hair appeared to be a combination of various mismatched tones, as if coloured by someone who was trying to use up the remains from a number of near-empty tubes. Moreover, her hair, though once gathered and piled high on her head, was slumping like a fancy cake that had been left in the sun. The flowers that had adorned various parts of her head now drooped and hung about her ears as if taking a short break.

There was a crunch of gravel and Jacob had crossed the car-park and stood before the second groom, his hand shading his eyes from the low sun, which fell directly on his face. 'What's your name?' he asked. The other groom pretended not to have heard, emitting only a loud burp by way of reply. Jacob stood quietly, reminding Edwin of a teacher waiting for a troublesome student to settle down. His continued silence seemed to have the desired effect because seconds later his antagonist began to shuffle, repeating, 'What?' in a voice that sounded increasingly petulant. 'What? What do you want, mate?'

Jacob simply shook his head and maintained his silence as the other groom's companions began to shift uneasily and look around. 'What?' asked the second groom for perhaps the fourth or fifth time. Then, speaking very slowly and clearly, Jacob murmured, 'I want you and your mates to piss off.' The second groom laughed. Hearing Jacob speak increased his confidence. He had found himself back on familiar ground. Smirking, he responded, 'We were here first, so you piss off.'

The childish remark filled Edwin with a sense of irritation. It had been a long day and he still had the drive back to Dunedin ahead of him. He wasn't sure what would happen next but he anticipated that things might get nasty. Instinctively he turned towards Matilda, half expecting her to step forward to intervene, but was surprised to see that she had wandered off and was scuffing through a pile of yellow leaves beneath a row of tall poplar trees at the far end of the carpark. Bending to gather leaves in her hands, she raised them to her face and breathed deeply, inhaling their earthy smell before allowing them to drift slowly to the ground. As they fell, some of the leaves caught and settled on her dark blue dress and these she examined with intense interest, her lips curving into a slight smile as she held them up to her nose. Edwin frowned, annoyed with himself for not having his camera ready to capture the only unguarded expression she had so far permitted herself.

He was aware of Jacob's voice, the second groom's response and eventually the raised voice of the other bride, shouting at them both to cut it out and behave like adults. And then, suddenly, the group fell quiet. Half expecting to witness someone pushed to the ground, Edwin swivelled around in time to catch sight of the woman moving to a spot only a few inches from Jacob, her voice stuttering, 'Jacob? Jacob Cook?' She hesitated, leant forward as if short-sighted, then continued, 'It is you, isn't it?'

An uneasy silence followed as the men from the second wedding group glanced from their bride to Jacob, waiting for him to explain. 'Yeah, my name's Jacob.' He spoke slowly, wary of saying anything that might lead him into the unknown territory suggested by the woman. He kept his eyes on her, however, and after a few more seconds he began to smile uncertainly. 'That's not your usual hair, is it?' It was clumsy but it seemed to meet with a degree of success because the girl smiled now, saying, 'It was blue the last time you saw me, if that helps.' A puzzled look came over Jacob's face, followed slowly by one of recognition. 'Jennifer?' he asked. 'Jen?' He stared a moment longer, then ran his hands through his hair. 'You look so different! You're not wearing glasses any more.'

Now it was the other groom's turn to look disconcerted. 'Jacob?' he said. 'Jacob – not that Jacob? This jerk is the guy whose name is tattooed on your bum?' he asked, his voice rising shrilly. From the exchange of glances between Jacob and Jennifer it was clear, even to Edwin, that this indeed was that Jacob. 'This is the Jacob,' continued the second groom, a note of panic in his voice, 'with the commitment problem? The one who dumped you when you told him you wanted to get married? This ugly bastard is Jacob?'

A brief discussion then began: two disparate conversations. The first took place between Jennifer and Jacob as they began to catch up on events of the past few years: the lengthy period spent by Jennifer in London, the eighteen months during which Jacob had toured Asia and Australia – where he had hooked up with Matilda – before returning to New Zealand.

Murmuring in the background, as Jennifer and Jacob spoke, was the increasingly indignant voice of the second groom, Luke, who was telling his friends about the videos Jennifer had allowed Jacob to make. 'They're sick,' he kept repeating, as he described how Jacob had set up a video camera in the bedroom and then recorded them having sex. 'You could see everything,' Luke complained. 'That guy is a real sicko, if you ask me. He's a real perv . . .' He frowned, oblivious to the leers on his companions' faces.

Edwin, however, could read their expressions, their imitations of sympathetic disgust no match for the stream of questions that probed for more and clearer detail. 'You mean,' said one, trying to contain a smirk, 'he filmed himself giving her one?'

'And you saw it all?' interrupted the second, unable to conceal the note of excitement in his voice.

'Like, did he film her touching herself?' continued the first, exchanging a glance with his friend. As the groom nodded gravely, both friends mumbled their condemnation, eyeing Jennifer up and down as they did so.

Suddenly, unaware of the conversation that had taken place

only a few feet from where she stood, Jennifer's voice broke a momentary silence, announcing, 'Yeah, I'd really love to have kids. A gang of boys . . . they're so sweet and cute. How about you?' Edwin waited, curious to hear Jacob's reply. 'Yeah, I would have liked to have kids. But it's not going to happen . . .' Something in his tone was so final that it took Edwin by surprise. It must have had a similar effect on Jennifer, too, because despite her quizzical glance she didn't push for detail but talked more about herself. 'Four or five boys' – though, of course, she'd be just as happy with girls. 'Boys don't give you as much grief as girls,' she explained. 'They're less complicated, aren't they? They're just like babies.'

Back and forth, the conversations continued, Edwin grasping snippets from both while all the time growing more and more impatient, eager to get on with his work and back to Dunedin.

Eventually Jacob said, 'Let's have a drink when we're finished here. What do you reckon?' In making his invitation, he appeared to have forgotten about both Matilda and Luke, the latter of whom now slouched against the bonnet of his car, firing hostile glances in Jacob's direction. But then, apparently having a change of heart, Luke answered for Jennifer: 'Yeah, okay mate. Might as well, I suppose.' It was arranged: as soon as Jacob and Matilda had finished their photos, they would meet the other party inside the tasting room and have a few wines. Edwin sighed with relief. At least he could now get on with his work.

Glancing back to where he had last seen Matilda, Edwin started. In her hands she held a video camera and was filming a pile of leaves that covered her feet. What on earth is she doing? He kept his eyes on her, noting that she was completely absorbed in the task at hand: filming leaves. He smiled. If she really was filming leaves – and that was how it looked to him – there was something quite delightful about it. He allowed himself to continue watching, taking an almost guilty pleasure in observing her. She was oblivious to his gaze. He noticed that she appeared quite at ease with the video camera. Unlike most amateurs, she didn't once lower it to check the controls. Neither did she at any point replay what she had filmed. It was as if she knew exactly what she wanted to record and was confident of her skill. Unexpectedly, he felt drawn to her in that moment, experiencing a kind of professional pride in her abilities.

He was still watching when, from behind he heard a male voice remark, 'Looks like the old video thing is still going on.'

'Yeah,' responded his friend, sniggering. Affronted, Edwin spun around, taking in the two groomsmen who stood watching Matilda. He scowled at them but neither took any notice. 'Pity she's so scrawny,' continued the first. 'I could probably go for her – if she had a bit more meat on her.'

'Yeah,' agreed the second. 'Not much of an arse.'

'No tits either,' added the first. 'Still, I wouldn't say no to a private viewing,' he concluded, nodding towards the camera.

Edwin was appalled. The private moment he had allowed himself to enjoy was instantly shattered. He felt he should step in immediately and put the youths in their place, but even as he prepared to say something he knew there was no point. Men of that age were not going to pay attention to him. Nevertheless, he heard himself scold them, telling them to show some respect for the bride. As he had anticipated, they responded to his reprimand with laughter.

He glanced back towards Matilda who, thankfully, was still filming leaves, unaware of the small drama that was taking place.

As he watched, she kicked her feet, sending yellow poplar leaves flying into the air. She followed their short flight with her camera and then repeated the process twice more before lowering the recorder and glancing over to Jacob. Following her gaze, Edwin also turned to Jacob, who was deep in conversation with Jennifer. Focused on Jennifer, Jacob, too, had missed the discussion that had taken place between the two groomsmen. Edwin turned back to his own camera and shook his head. It was none of his business. Even so, he couldn't help thinking, That marriage won't last a year.

I remember the way Matilda said, 'I have to do this, I'm sorry.' As she kissed me, I felt bewildered, baffled. It was as if I'd been standing at a counter waiting for my change when, instead of being handed $1.20 as I'd expected, I'd been given a $10 bill. My brain instantly became muddled – the money wasn't mine, I should give it back, and yet I could just as easily press the crumpled bill into my pocket and say nothing. Matilda kissed me and in my confusion I didn't know how to respond – so I fumbled. I got it wrong. I missed that first opportunity and I made a mess of things. I'm sorry.

TWO

Edwin sat in his living room, drinking from his cup of tea. The room hadn't changed much in all the years he'd owned his house. The wallpaper was a green bamboo print, chosen by him in the sixties because he liked plants but had never had any luck with real ones, the kind that needed watering or re-potting. He still liked the wallpaper; being surrounded by the tall shoots calmed him after a long day in the studio. In real life, he'd never seen bamboo like it but he thought that somewhere, China perhaps, it might grow like that. There must be at least one country in the world, he thought, where bamboo grows tall and green, where every shoot is distinct from its neighbour yet rustles as the wind passes through. He'd like to visit that country.

He turned his attention from the bamboo to the wall opposite him. It was a wall he referred to as 'The wall of strays'. Pinned to it – because he wouldn't consider having the photographs framed – were images that had not been collected from him. Photographs that had been commissioned and paid for but then abandoned, for reasons he never knew. There were many photographs, some dating back to the early sixties and others that had been taken as recently as a month ago. He liked examining the pictures; there were many things that caught his eye. Some things were obvious: the expressions on the sitters' faces or their clothing, for example. However, some features were not so apparent – things that might go unnoticed by a casual visitor. Not only had the earlier photographs faded from the sun that fell in broad sweeps across the wall, but the colours of the prints themselves had changed over the years. The pictures taken in the sixties appeared golden, for example, whereas the more recent prints were slightly blue in tone. He had changed film brands several times and he could detect that in the colours. Kodak was warm, summery, whereas Fuji was cool, elegant: good for blondes or outdoor types, those with weathered skin who could appear ruddy no matter how carefully he arranged the studio lights.

He remembered the people depicted in the photographs. All of them. Most of them he hadn't liked, particularly. That was the odd thing about all this – the fact that he papered his wall with images of people he hadn't much cared for. The people he did get on with tended to collect their photographs; they were happy with the results and the circumstances that had led to their being taken in the first place. The pictures surrounding him, however, represented the dissatisfied, the reluctant, even the hostile. People he had had to cajole into sitting for the camera: divorced couples who nevertheless continued the habit of having an annual family portrait taken, graduation photographs of people who had dropped out of university but were too scared to admit their failure to their parents, photographs of extended families – people who weren't even talking to each other when they entered the studio. He remembered sessions that ended with someone – the youngest son, usually – erupting, 'Fuck this. This is bullshit!' before storming out. And of course there were engagement photographs belonging to couples who never got married.

Some of the photographs represented lifestyles he didn't quite understand. A photograph of two middle-aged men in leather holding hands, another of a woman in her mid-forties wearing a lacy camisole and frilly panties. The boy in his teens, naked from the waist up, a large tattoo of a tank across his chest, the inscription 'Don't give up the fight!' running across his abdomen. These people mirrored the changes that had taken place in his business. Beginning in the late seventies, the small family businesses that had been his neighbours for years had slowly begun to disappear. The drapery was the first to go, followed by the watchmaker, the family business specialising in school uniforms, and the locksmith. Taking their place were a mortgage broker, a television rental company and a luggage shop, and then, when they relocated, a tattoo parlour, a shop supplying 'legal highs' and smoking paraphernalia, and finally a 'boutique' with painted windows that initially traded under the name Through the Keyhole but more recently became Adult Entertainment and Sex Toys.

It was the latter business that sent him customers. It had taken him by surprise at first, the middle-aged, slightly downtrodden people who would arrive in his studio, mumbling requests for something exotic but tasteful. Often it would be older women wanting to show a side of them that had gone unnoticed by their husbands for years. Behind a curtain in his back room they would shuffle out of elastic-waisted trackpants and teal sweatshirts and reappear heavily made up and dressed in red or black lace, their décolletage red and mottled from years of sun exposure, their thighs dimpled and showing traces of varicose veins, their ankles thick and perhaps decorated with a small rose tattoo as they tottered to the centre of the studio on fur-trimmed mules.

As he set up the camera, aware of their eyes watching his every move, Edwin would try not to imagine what thoughts were going through their heads, the events that had led them to this moment: the hope or desperation that had brought them to him in the belief that the photograph he would take would somehow make them feel more loved, more desired, happier within themselves. He would smile at them and yet avoid making eye contact until he was safely positioned behind the camera. He recognised the fragility of the moment: that if he was too friendly, too familiar, or even too admiring, their persona would crumble and they would be left feeling self-conscious and humiliated. Instead, he worked quietly, professionally, taking extra care to adjust the lighting so as to draw attention away from the shadows around their eyes, the drooping skin hanging from their upper arms, the folds around the stomach that no amount of restrained breathing or rigid posture could correct. The cellulite was easier to disguise; even the veins posed little problem, but the dullness in their eyes was another matter. He would see them smile for the camera and his heart would ache. In their expression was the acknowledgement of failure: times that had passed, all that had left them long ago, days they could not recapture.

From his seat by the table he gazed now at the most recent addition to his collection. The photograph taken only a month ago, of Jacob and Matilda. It was a good photograph, a remarkably clear image, nicely composed, both subjects looking straight at the camera. It was a shame Matilda wasn't smiling but she looked pretty, all the same. It was the last photograph of his career, a fact he had to keep reminding himself of. He was now officially retired.

It had been odd that first morning, waking at seven and knowing he could choose when to get up. For a moment or two he had felt fragmented, almost weightless – as if the breeze entering through his open bedroom window might gather him up and carry him away. A sensation of slight panic went through him and in order to calm down he had to tell himself he could call in to the studio, just briefly, to see how his neighbour's son, Simon, was coping on his first day as the new owner of the business. He knew, even as the idea occurred to him, that Simon didn't need his help. He was capable of looking after himself and would probably appreciate being on his own, free from Edwin's watchful eye. Simon was a good kid, full of ideas. He was going to turn the business around – make it funkier, more up to date, while at the same time acknowledging the retro nature of a photography studio. These were Simon's words, not Edwin's. The entrance area, redecorated in a sixties patterned wallpaper with a red vinyl couch and a kidney-shaped table, would act as a meeting place, a space where photographer and client could discuss the kind of image they wished to create. There would be more communication; the relationship between the photographer and the sitter would resemble that of an architect and client: a creative, two-way process aimed at getting a result favourable to both parties.

As well as photography, Simon would offer a video service for weddings and family gatherings – as well as classes in digital photography and video editing.

He had the skills to do all of these things and he was a hard worker. More than that, he had a good head for business. He had already approached the adult entertainment boutique next door, outlining the services he could offer their clients. Discretion and a twenty per cent discount for cash. He had smiled as he shook the hand of the man who sat in the back room, a stack of magazines pushed to one side, boxes of vibrators and dildos lying scattered across the floor. Scarcely had Simon introduced himself to the adult entertainment market than he was doing the rounds of schools and daycare centres, handing out pamphlets offering family portraits and 'First day at school' specials – three prints for the price of one! 'Goodness,' remarked Edwin when he heard of Simon's promotional offers. 'Be careful, won't you? I'd hate to see the photos mixed up – imagine the fuss it would cause!'

'Fuss?' laughed Simon. 'It would be a nightmare! My face would be flashed across the papers, hauled before the television news before the prints had even dried . . .' He hesitated then, a look of amusement crossing his face, causing Edwin a moment's panic.

'You mustn't,' stuttered Edwin. 'It would be the end of you.'

Simon had continued to smile for a moment longer, weighing up the publicity benefits of such an unfortunate 'accident', but then he'd frowned, shaken his head and murmured, 'Yes, you're right. It would be a disaster.' A sigh of relief had escaped from Edwin and then they'd both laughed. It was too dreadful to contemplate.

Edwin glanced back to the image of Jacob and Matilda. He wondered what had happened to them, why they hadn't collected their photographs. Perhaps, he concluded, they were still on their honeymoon, but even as the thought entered his head, he knew it wasn't true. Most newlyweds were so eager to collect their pictures they would be waiting outside the studio, two steps behind him as he unlocked the door and walked into the back room. It was most unusual – unless something had gone wrong – for wedding photographs to go uncollected.

He tilted his head, his eyes still fixed on the photograph, and stared. There was nothing remarkable about the image – it was simply a competently taken photograph of a soon-to-be-married couple – but, he realised, there was something contained in the expression of the young woman that he was sure he had seen before. He searched her face for some clue as to what it might be, but when nothing came to mind he turned away, picking up the book he had been reading and continuing from the place he had left off – or, rather, fallen asleep during – the night before.

From time to time, as he turned a page, he would glance back to the photograph, hoping against hope that he would see whatever it was he was looking for; that he would remember what it was. He had to concede, however, that his memory – or perhaps it was just his brain – didn't always fulfil its potential. Politicians' names, song lyrics, grocery items . . . none of these things stuck in his mind any more. But that was not the worst of it. Bits and pieces had a way of popping into his head at the most random of moments. Often fleeting, like remnants of dreams, these memories would take him by complete surprise: he might be standing in the aisle of the supermarket, for example, trying to remember the things he had written on the shopping list he had left on the kitchen bench when, out of the blue, the name of the current Minister of Energy would enter his thoughts. The name would not remain with him, though, it would simply pass through, like some falling star drifting across the night sky: one minute a bright flash, the next nothing at all. If he was lucky – and sometimes he was – one thought would trigger off another. Remembering the Minister of Energy's name might, if it was a good day, remind him that he was out of porridge. But there was just as much chance that he would simply convince himself he was out of porridge and arrive home to discover that it was detergent that was missing from his cupboards; that he had enough porridge to last him for a month.

Most often he was able to accept these lapses in memory with good grace. He was growing older; it was natural to forget one or two things a day – it was no more troublesome than discovering more and more strands of hair caught in his comb each morning. So far, he had never forgotten anything of importance: he could still remember his childhood years spent with his father, Albert, at the TB sanatorium near Waipiata. Moreover, he could picture the way the furniture was arranged in the small brick house that was allocated to his father, the medical superintendent of the sanatorium. He could remember the last time he saw his mother, Jessie, Jess: the clear sunny day when she had bent to kiss him on the forehead as he climbed into the truck next to Samuel, the gardener, and drove in to Ranfurly to buy a new wheelbarrow. He could recall – or was it imagine? – the look that took possession of his father's face from that day on. An expression of complete bewilderment. He was no longer a young, neatly dressed, slim man who walked with an air of confidence through the wards but, from that day on, a man who appeared to have lost his way. He looked, remembered Edwin, not only abandoned but as if he had been stripped of everything he held dear.

When Edwin had returned from town, the wheelbarrow tied to the back of Samuel's truck, feeling happy and excited because he had been allowed to make the final choice between the wooden and metal one, he had discovered his father alone in his office, staring out of the window, a fountain pen gripped tightly between his fingers as ink leaked over his hand like blood from a wound. His father's appearance had scared him and he had run out, searching for his mother, seeking comfort in her arms. But she hadn't been there of course. She had left shortly after him, driven by a fellow nurse to the station, where she had sat and waited for three hours until a passing motor vehicle had stopped and offered a ride.

At the time, however, Edwin knew none of this. When he had heard his father say only, 'Your mother has gone,' he had assumed, from his father's expression, that she had 'gone' to the same place that all the seriously ill patients went: heaven. In the time it took for him to choose between two wheelbarrows his mother had 'gone' – she'd died. And it had never occurred to him, as a seven-year-old, to ask how. One look at his father's face told him all he needed to know. Seeing Albert's staring, empty eyes and his mouth that looked poised to slip off his face, Edwin knew something terrible must have happened. Although he would have liked to know what it was, he understood that it was far more important, now, to take care of his beloved father. Even as a seven-year-old he could see that his father needed protecting – and so, for as long as he could remember, he had never asked what had happened and his father had never offered to tell him. So, unbelievable though it now seemed, for more than fifty years Edwin had gone on assuming his mother was dead.

I remember the first time I touched Matilda. My actions surprised me. She was sitting next to me in the car and I had glanced across to her as I answered a question she had put to me. Something unimportant that I remember now only because of the fact that in the second I turned to her, I saw that she had a black speck on her cheek. I don't know why I didn't simply draw her attention to it. My car, after all, is reasonably new – there is a small vanity mirror mounted on the passenger sunshade. Instead, however, and to my embarrassment, I reached across and picked the speck from her cheek. It was an eyelash. I held it on my fingertip, looked at it and said, stupidly, 'It's an eyelash.' She nodded and then did something I did not anticipate. She blew gently on my finger and the eyelash disappeared, drifting to some hidden corner of the car. I blushed. In retrospect, I should have said nothing – or just told her she had something on her cheek. But, instead I had touched her and I retained that touch, that sensation of smooth skin, as I reached for the key in the ignition and started the car. Everything – even the steering wheel – felt softer, gentler. I had never been aware of my grip on the wheel before, but now I held it loosely, careful not to grasp it too tightly. I had touched her and felt her breath on my skin. For the first time.

THREE

Edwin realised with a start that he had been waiting for the weekend before beginning his trip. The working week was such a part of him that he couldn't, even now, imagine beginning a holiday on a Tuesday. He smiled. Even the terminology was wrong. He wasn't going on holiday – he was simply going away. His first trip away that was not defined, or limited, by work. It was strange, the unfamiliarity of such freedom. He could come and go as he pleased – whenever he wanted. A sense of excitement took hold of him, a kind of giddy light-headedness – a freedom from anxiety. Even when he left school he had not experienced such a sensation.

Back then he had followed the path gently laid out for him by his father. Recognising that his son was reluctant to follow in his footsteps and enter medicine, his father had, nevertheless, used what connections he had to secure Edwin a position at the medical school, training as an assistant to the chief medical photographer.

It had been an altogether peculiar start to a career in photography: trailing his colleague from department to department, setting up shots of gangrenous limbs, hydatid cysts, skin diseases, misshapen appendages and so forth. Image after image of diseased and distressed patients that seemed, in Edwin's mind, to reinforce the lack of control people had over their own lives. The woman with the goitre who, for years, had worn an amber necklace in the hope that she might cure herself; the young cross-eyed boy who cried with terror at the idea of corrective surgery; the elderly diabetic who kept looking at the ground, his eyes fixed on the empty space directly below the dangling stump of his recently amputated leg . . . all these people shared a look of bewilderment and fear. Perhaps a few of them retained an expression of hope but some, the most severely afflicted – like the girl who had been burnt when her nightdress caught fire – were no longer able to convey any feelings through facial expression. People like her were lifelike rather than alive. Edwin was drawn to their faces because part of his job had been to blank out their eyes with a thick black oblong, to render them anonymous. Whatever human or individual dignity they retained had to be erased – an act that pained him.

None of these photographs adorned his 'wall of strays'. They were too private, too stark.

As Edwin walked around his house, gathering together items of clothing, toiletries and books, he found himself thinking more and more about what he was planning to do. It had taken him years to reach this point – too many years, probably – and why he had left it so long was difficult to explain, even to himself. The only reason he could think of was that he hadn't felt ready before. The time had never seemed right; he had too many other things to take care of: his business, his vegetable garden . . . commitments. He smiled. The excuses sounded feeble – but then why did he imagine he needed excuses? He didn't need to explain himself – least of all to himself.

He wouldn't even be making this trip if, during one of his visits to Dr Aubrey's surgery a full eight years ago, he hadn't picked up a Chinese-language magazine and flicked through the pages, glancing at the pictures and the incomprehensible text as he filled in the minutes before his appointment. Why he chose that magazine and not one of the many other outdated monthlies was a mystery to him. He hadn't even really noticed that the magazine was written in Chinese until he was halfway through, so slight was the attention he paid to the words. But he remembered, very clearly, the moment he saw the photograph of a small group of people standing on the ice at Franz Josef Glacier. It had been remarkable – the briefest glimpse of a picture as he turned the page had nevertheless stopped him dead in his tracks.

He recalled the way his heart had started pounding, a powerful thump, thump, thump that undoubtedly sent his blood pressure rocketing – a fact that would be remarked upon by Dr Aubrey a few minutes later. As Edwin had sat back in his chair, he had found himself glancing at the other patients in the waiting room as if expecting them to be staring at him, watching him, prompting him to turn back the page and take a second look at the photo. But that was the thing. He couldn't flick back. He was immobilised by the thought of what he had seen. Instead, he sat with the opened magazine on his lap, displaying an advertisement featuring a jar of Merino handcream before a background of green pastures and snow-capped mountains. 'Merino handcream' were the only words in English; the rest were a minefield of Chinese characters, little complex boxes and lines that meant nothing to him but that he kept looking at as his mind raced to recreate the photograph of the people posed on the glacier.

When his name was called out, he found he could barely stand. His legs wobbled and for an instant he thought he might topple, so unstable had he felt. He stumbled after the nurse, the corner of the magazine clutched in his hand, the pages flapping and one falling to the ground by his feet – a page he was told not to worry about; the nurse would pick it up, which she did, immediately screwing it up into a ball and tossing it into a waste-paper basket.

Edwin followed her into the doctor's room and only as he sat down, smoothing the pages of the magazine out on his knee, did he permit himself to turn back the page to look once more at the picture of the trampers. He searched their faces, then, looking up, addressed Dr Aubrey: 'I think my mother's alive after all.' It was a statement that invited confirmation but, never having seen Edwin's mother, Dr Aubrey was unable to provide it. Instead he looked from the photograph to Edwin and back again, then sighed, a long, slow expulsion of breath, murmuring, 'It's possible, I suppose.' For minutes they sat in silence and then, remembering where he was, Edwin glanced up once more, adding feebly, 'I thought she was dead. I always assumed she had died – long ago.'

He was grateful that Dr Aubrey hadn't brushed his remarks aside, or hurried him along. He was even more thankful that the doctor hadn't reached for his stethoscope and begun to take his blood pressure. Instead they sat side by side, two middle-aged men, while Edwin recounted the story of his childhood, his mother's abrupt disappearance and his father's bewildered heartbreak and inability to speak about his wife, the woman he loved beyond all else.

Edwin had felt the need to explain why he, himself, had never before mentioned his mother to the doctor. He had the feeling that his failure to raise the topic so much as once in all those years might strike the doctor as some kind of stupidity and he wanted to make it clear that it wasn't lack of curiosity that had led him to keep quiet all these years, but the fact that he loved his father dearly and had wanted to protect him and not cause him any more pain.

Speaking to Dr Aubrey about such personal matters embarrassed him because it highlighted the bizarre way he had handled his life – the fact that he had never tried to find out what had happened to his mother. That he could have let her slip away through an exaggerated sensitivity to his father's feelings. It was stupid, he now realised, but he had believed his mother was dead – he truly had.

Edwin and Dr Aubrey sat quietly, the doctor at his desk, Edwin on the chair next to the hard examination bed – the place he always sat. He was aware of the ticking of the second hand on the electric clock on the wall. Whatever else, his hearing and eyesight were still in excellent working order. It was only his heart that needed attention – but even so, it had never failed him. True, it wasn't as strong as it could be – but it still worked, ticking away, from one breath to the next.

'My mother was born with a harelip – it was one of the first things people noticed about her. It's funny but I never paid much attention to it. She had a scar and her top lip was kind of twisted but that was all. Yet a memory, or an image, of the way her mouth appeared must have remained with me all these years . . . how else could I have identified her after all this time?'

The doctor shrugged, and looked once more at the magazine page that was opened in front of him. 'It's not unusual that you wouldn't have paid attention to her lip when you were a child. You probably saw her in a different light to most people. She was your mother, after all.'

'Yes,' replied Edwin quietly, but as he spoke he felt increasingly agitated, almost impatient with Dr Aubrey for not *seeing* the lip. His mother's scarred lip, the strange, determined way she held her mouth was his only evidence – the only thing that had led him to believe that the woman in the photograph was the woman he had not seen for years. The doctor had to see it too. If he didn't, the whole case might fall apart. The woman in the photograph might not be his mother but someone else's.

'When was your mother born?' asked Dr Aubrey.

'Around 1925, I think,' responded Edwin. 'I'm not sure exactly, but sometime in the early twenties . . .'

'So,' continued Dr Aubrey, 'she was probably seventy-one years old when this photograph was taken. That's right, isn't it? The magazine is dated 1996. It's two years old – so let's say she's around seventy-three now. Give or take.'

Edwin felt his throat tighten. He sensed the doubt in Dr Aubrey's manner and he imagined his voice sounding like that of a seven-year-old as he tried to protest: It's her. I know it is. I know it's her. But instead he nodded dumbly and asked if he could keep the magazine.

Eight years had gone by. Edwin smiled to himself. He'd always suspected he was slow to act on things, that he needed time to think things through, but in pursuing the matter of his mother he had been exceptionally cautious, even by his own standards. No, that wasn't fair. He had done a lot of thinking in the past eight years – and, he had to admit, a bit of research. He had been uncertain about what he had seen. Deep down, he doubted that he could identify his mother from a single photograph. After all, he had been seven when he last saw her, and he had not laid eyes on her since. She had been in her twenties when she left the sanatorium – surely he couldn't recognise a face, even his mother's, after all that time.

But in the eight years since finding the magazine picture he had convinced himself that he actually could recognise her image. And whenever he needed proof he would reach for his wallet – a soft brown leather billfold that his father had given him for his twenty-first birthday – and open it and gaze for minutes on end at the only other photograph he had of her: one taken in 1950. It had been taken in the garden of their house. Visible in the background were the buildings of the sanatorium, solid brick with a long covered veranda turned to capture the sun and breeze.

In the photograph, his mother, Jessie, stood next to a sunflower. The sunflower was as tall as her – taller, in fact. He remembered the sunflower as clearly as he pictured his mother: it was the only one in the garden and it was his – he had grown it. It was important, that fact: that the flower was his. He had felt proud and possessive of it, measuring and comparing its height against his own and that of any visitors who came to the house. The flower towered above him. It was taller than both his mother and his father. In such a dry, barren, *healthy* landscape that flower had stood out like a lighthouse, a kind of beacon. That's how he imagined it. A light shining over the burnt-dry beds that made up his father's garden. It had been his, that sunflower – just as his mother had been his.

He knew now that that photograph would have been the last one taken of his mother before she left. He hadn't known that at the time, of course, but perhaps she had. Often he would find himself searching her expression for some indication of foreknowledge – a hint that she knew she was about to leave and that Edwin and the sunflower would not be joining her. Sometimes he wondered if his mother was excited at the prospect of her departure. Was she pleased to be leaving him? Was she so fed up with living in the sanatorium that she couldn't wait for the day when, bags packed, she could hurry off to the station, never to return? What, wondered Edwin, was she looking forward to? A life of freedom – one without responsibilities for a child, without ties to a husband who was so keenly aware of his position as medical superintendent that he had become embedded in his duties, unable to join her for fear of letting his patients down.

At times Edwin imagined his mother as a fiercely independent woman: one of those ladies who embarked on a grand overseas journey, travelling alone to minute tropical islands in order to capture exotic insects or convert savages. For some reason he also imagined her as a mountain climber – which, unbelievably, turned out to be far closer to the truth than he could have anticipated. He pictured her wearing knee-breeches and boots as she scaled Mt Cook and looked down from the summit towards the open countryside of the Mackenzie Basin or the green rich hills of the West Coast. In his mind's eye she breathed deeply and smiled, revelling in her strength and the beauty of her surroundings.

There were times, however, when Edwin perceived a different expression in his mother's eyes. One of a deeply troubled young woman, a woman who looked ashamed and yet somehow decisive. She appeared as if she had been struggling with some internal monster for years but had finally reached a decision – a decision which, however, brought little relief, perhaps only a vague sense of hope. He was drawn once more to her mouth, tracing with his fingertip the scar that curved from her top lip to her nostril. The scar was so pronounced in the photo he held, its curve contrasting so starkly with the straight line made by her unsmiling lips.

The truth was, Edwin had no idea what his mother had been thinking. He had no idea. Moreover, he knew nothing about her – nothing at all.

No, that was not quite correct. He did know something – a small fragment of information gleaned from the article written in Chinese that he had happened upon in Dr Aubrey's waiting room. One evening, after closing his studio for the night, he had wandered down to his local fish and chip shop and made his usual request for three fish and one scoop of chips. He had sat on a plastic outdoor chair near the counter as he had struggled with the thoughts that ran through his head, staging an internal battle over whether or not he should ask May, the woman who for years had been serving him his regular Thursday-night meal, to translate the article for him. As he sat, waiting for his dinner to cook, he had played and replayed the arguments over and over again. If he got the article translated he would have to trace his mother. He couldn't have it translated and then leave it at that. That option would be impossible. The moment he knew what the article said, a whole series of motions would clunk into place and he would have to keep pace with them, journeying from one fragment of information to the next. The problem was, he wasn't sure that he was ready to make that journey. Even though eight years had passed since he had laid eyes on the magazine, he was still unwilling to make that commitment.

If he didn't get the article translated he could go home and watch *Coronation Street* and spend this evening like any other. He could just sit peacefully and not do anything. Every now and then he could bring the article out and look at the photograph and wonder what the piece of writing said – he could even create his own version of the story – and then he would be able to put the magazine down and go back to watching television or reading a book or looking at the photographs pinned to his 'wall of strays'.

The one thing that always caught him – that drifted back and forth above him like a fishing net skimmed across the surface of a pond – was the knowledge that if he didn't get the article translated he would never know what it said. In fact, what he most wanted was to know what the article said, but then be allowed to un-know it again, so that whatever was written wouldn't haunt him. That was what he wanted: the right to simultaneously find out and forget the information.

It had taken months of Thursdays before he eventually got the article translated. He hadn't arrived at the fish and chip shop with that intention, but it had been a peculiar week, a week in which nothing had gone to plan. It had not even been a Thursday, he recalled, when he placed his order for three fish and a scoop of chips. It was a Tuesday. He had arrived early, just after five, and when he entered the shop May was sitting on the plastic chair rubbing her calves while her daughter, Nancy, worked behind the counter, pre-frying chips for the night's customers. Seeing May sitting down he had suddenly realised she was an old woman. He had never noticed it before, but now, for the first time in his life, he took in her black hair streaked with grey, her sallow skin and her sunken eyes. For a second longer than was polite, he found himself staring at her and it was only her voice that jolted him out of his dream. 'Mr Edwin,' she laughed, 'your wife not cook for you tonight?'

It was a small thing – an off-the-cuff remark, no more than a joke, really – but in hearing May utter that small sentence Edwin was struck dumb. He had, he realised, been frequenting this chip shop every week for as long as he could remember, and for all that time May had assumed he was married. Despite the fact that they saw each other every week, they knew nothing about each other. Perhaps he knew more about her – her family did work alongside her, after all – but she clearly knew nothing about him. She didn't even know he was not married, had never been married – that his father was dead, that he had no siblings and a mother he could barely remember. For a second he felt stricken. It was as if he had suddenly seen himself for what he was: a man completely alone in the world, unloved by anyone – a kind of shapeless, weightless orphan. He had no connections – to anyone. He was a remnant, or something else, some other shredded scrap – he didn't know what.

He found himself smiling at May, nodding his head as if by simply pretending to have a wife he might somehow feel more substantial. But he felt slightly dizzy and in that moment, without being conscious of having made any decision, he found himself pulling the magazine from his briefcase and passing it to May and, in a faint voice, asking her to read the article to him.

I haven't told anyone this before. After my mother left, my father would come into my bedroom every evening to say goodnight. He never missed a night. Never. No matter how busy he was, he was always there – like a well-dressed shadow, I used to think. He would sit on the edge of my bed and look down at me and smile and say, 'Night and bless.' And then he would sit for a few minutes looking at my face. I think now that he was trying to see my mother. He was searching for some resemblance, some flicker in my expression that would bring her back to him. That's what I think he was doing. Often, though, I would close my eyes and just lie still and I would feel his hand reach out and stroke my hair, and I would feel him kiss me very gently and he would say, 'I love you,' and I would imagine that it was not him in my room, but her. He touched me so gently that I would persuade myself she had come back. Sometimes, I would be so sure my mother had returned that after a few seconds I would open my eyes wide . . . and there would be my father, his eyes tightly closed, lost in thought, still stroking my hair.

FOUR

Two thoughts entered Edwin's mind in quick succession. The first, that after all this time, he had finally started out on his journey to trace his mother. The second, that his decision to seek out Matilda's house might appear odd.

When he'd left his house earlier in the day he'd simply remembered he still had her photographs and that he would be passing through Ranfurly, where she lived, later that day. It had seemed very straightforward – a kind of practical arrangement: she had paid for the photos and he was in a position to drop them off without going to any inconvenience – or cost. But as he stood at her gate, he wondered why he hadn't couriered the photos out to her weeks before – and then he began to feel uncertain. Suddenly he worried that perhaps he had promised to send the pictures but had forgotten about it. It was quite possible Matilda would respond to his gesture not with gratitude but with anger; she might very well feel annoyed with him for taking so long with her wedding pictures. For a second, Edwin considered going back to his car, driving to the local post shop and sending the photographs from there, but then he decided he was being ridiculous. What did it matter, really? He'd retired, he was giving her the photographs she – or Jacob, rather – had paid for. End of story, as people said.

As he approached the front door he hoped she wouldn't be home. It would be easier to leave the pictures and just go. He could put them in a safe place – on the couch or table he could see on the veranda – and then he could leave and go about his other business, his real reason for being in this part of the country. It was only as he made his way up the garden path that it dawned on him that it was unusual for so much furniture to be outside. Not only was there a couch and a table but also several chairs and, oddest of all, a piano. The gardens of student flats back in Dunedin were often surrounded, he knew, by random pieces of furniture, but it was unusual to see a piano included in the mess.

The TB sanatorium had had a piano. An old upright, very plain, with the words 'Wallis' and 'London' in gold on the underside of its lid. He'd never learnt how to play. He was entirely without musical talent – a surprising fact given that both his father and mother were such competent musicians. It was his mother who excelled at the piano, while his father often accompanied her on the violin. His father's fingers, he remembered, were well suited to the violin: they were long and tapered. For some reason Edwin thought they looked European. It must have been because his father's hands were so unlike those of any of the patients in the sanatorium. Even the weakest, most poorly of men had hands that retained a memory of strength. He remembered how the hands of the men, palms flat against laundered white sheets, would catch his eye as he walked through the wards in search of his father. It wasn't the men's worn faces, their tired expressions that would move him, but their hands. Even as a boy of ten he saw in their large, immobile hands an indication of what had been lost – a life that had been compromised by the onset of disabling disease. It was the hands that suffered – that was what he thought back then. The hands that grieved for a former life: a useful life.

Music hands, piano hands – and most of all violin hands – were different. They could adapt to a change in circumstance. They could turn the tissue-like pages of a book, take a needle and thread and embroider a handkerchief, darn a sock or mend a tear in a shirt . . . but those men's hands were useless when taken out of their environment. They knew no other purpose than to haul bales of hay, cut wood or grab a sheep roughly by its scruff, directing it one way or the other through the pens. The hands of those men had no idea what to do in a clean, airy ward, so they remained motionless on the turned-down sheets, as idle as two working dogs chained to a kennel on a late summer evening.

Standing on the veranda before the wedged-open door, Edwin tapped gently on the keys of the piano. Although he could not play, he knew one or two tunes well enough for them to be recognisable. They were songs his mother had taught him. It was funny – he hadn't thought about them for years, though he would hear them occasionally on the radio, often during the Saturday-night request show on National Radio, where people from one town or country would contact distant friends and family members in another – the music forming a bridge across the ocean that separated them. 'I'm thinking of you. I haven't written for a long time. We're all fine over here. How are you? You must remember this . . . ?' The fragment of their greeting contained in three minutes of Vera Lynn, Flanagan and Allen or that Canadian – well, he assumed he was Canadian, the performer with the rich, deep voice. What was his name? Edwin asked himself, annoyed once more at having come across something so familiar and yet so far out of his reach. He hummed snippets of tunes to himself but the Canadian's name continued to elude him. It was strange but he felt he could picture the performer – although, in truth, he had never seen a photograph of him. In his mind he could hear the voice: the mellow tone, a bit like Val Doonican's, a little like that other man whose name he had forgotten. But still he couldn't recall the name. What is his name? What was the song? My old Canadian home? My home? Canadian? Come on, Edwin, think!

His frustration was made worse by the fact that it was not a song his mother ever played – she preferred Chopin, Schubert and Debussy to any of the popular songwriters of the day. Had she stayed, Edwin might have developed a stronger interest in the piano. It was possible. A vague image came back to him: of himself sitting on his mother's knee while she played Debussy's 'Clair de Lune'. He recalled the warmth of her body against his back, the way he snuggled into her as if she was an armchair moulded, through frequent use, to the contours of his body. He remembered watching her fingers as they glided over the keys – how he imagined them as butterflies, or spiders . . . butterflies for 'Clair de Lune', spiders for Chopin's 'Valse', a dying moth for the 'Moonlight Sonata'. He would shadow her movements, anticipate where her fingers would alight next, which key, what note – he sometimes rested his hands gently on the backs of his mother's own as she traced the keyboard. His small hands on her larger ones – his black-rimmed, chewed fingernails; her creamy skin, tapered fingers, round, sugar-almond nails. His hands touching hers, pretending that they were hers, that they were two halves brought together . . . that they would remain so until he was a grown man.

Out of the corner of his eye Edwin caught a slight movement. Someone was watching him. He glanced up and immediately recognised the girl, Matilda. She stood at the far end of the long central hallway. Although he knew she had seen him, and that she must have heard him playing, she showed no signs of acknowledgement and made no move to walk towards him. It was difficult to see her clearly. Although he stood on the veranda, he was not shaded by it, and his eyes strained against the bright light around him as he peered through the open door into the darkness of the hallway. Feeling increasingly awkward, he stepped forward and tapped on the door – a light knock, the kind of self-conscious knock visitors make when they can hear or see the occupant is home. A knock intended not to cause offence.

Edwin was taken aback when Matilda made no response. He felt confused by her lack of reaction. It was almost as if she was waging some internal battle, trying to decide whether or not she wanted to see him, hovering in indecision – afraid, perhaps of what she could see in his hands. Surely she had guessed that he had the photographs. In his confusion, Edwin found that his thoughts had begun to drift; instead of focusing on his next move he found himself thinking about Nova Scotia, something to do with Nova Scotia. He frowned, perplexed at the way his brain appeared to be able to take off on its own, setting its own course. My Nova Scotia home. Of course, 'My Nova Scotia Home' – that was the song title!

He hesitated, waiting for the performer's name to follow and glanced at Matilda, as if expecting her to tell him. Then he noticed that a ray of light from the open door had seeped towards her, lighting her feet and the hem of her dress. It was midnight blue. Her wedding dress. As if conscious of the light, Matilda abruptly took a step, retreating further from the doorway and into the shadow. She hesitated for a moment and then, making her mind up, she walked down the passage towards him, hovering a few feet from the front door.

'I don't want them,' she said, suddenly breaking the silence, pointing to the large folder in Edwin's hands.

If he thought about it, Edwin had long ago reached the same conclusion – after all, if she'd wanted the photographs she would have collected them – but he nevertheless found himself responding, 'Oh!' as if surprised by her remark. He was, he realised, attempting to be polite. It would be wrong, in the situation, to respond, 'I thought you would say that.' He had to allow her to steer the conversation; it was up to her to draw him in – if she chose to do so.

'You were paid,' she continued after a moment's silence. Her voice was not one of accusation or defence, it was flat, almost expressionless. She was merely stating a fact. But, although she was not seeking it, Edwin found himself offering reassurance, 'Yes, they're all paid for.' He hesitated, then added, 'Don't worry, you're not the first one – there have been others. You're not the first client to decide to forgo the pictures.' He saw her raise her chin, a slight upwards nod of the head followed by a simple, 'Oh.'

His observation, however, appeared to have relaxed her. She no longer looked wary, and although she didn't smile, her face seemed to brighten slightly as if released from tension.

Edwin knew he could leave, that he could say goodbye and

take the photographs back with him – he could even throw them away now. Although she hadn't said as much, he felt certain he had Matilda's permission to do so. He had no desire to go chasing after the boy, Jacob. His job, as far as he was concerned, was finished: tied off like the bundles of newspapers he kept stacked in his garage. He lingered, however, his eyes roving over the pieces of furniture on the veranda, the piano, then back to the girl. He was aware that she was watching him; he heard her sigh and then ask, 'How long have you been playing?' Her voice was quiet, gentle, and for the first time Edwin thought he detected a slight accent – Australian, perhaps. He was about to reply but stopped, suddenly reticent. If he was to answer truthfully – and there was no reason why he shouldn't – he would have to say that he had been tinkering with the keys since the late 1940s. Instead, he replied, 'I started playing when I was around five or six.'

Matilda nodded and looked down at her toe, prodding at a torn fragment of newspaper with her foot. Then she spoke again, asking, 'Who taught you?' This time there was a boldness in her manner. Edwin recognised the tone: it was not unknown to him. In his experience, only the most taciturn of clients adopted it. It was their way of disguising their shyness; they would ask questions, talk too loudly or bluster – anything to divert the attention away from themselves. Matilda was doing it now, trying to hide behind a direct personal question. What's more, he realised, she was trying to give the impression that she didn't care. He felt sorry for her, so he clarified his earlier statement, saying, 'I began to play in 1949. My mother taught me.'

His answer, he soon guessed, made Matilda even more self-conscious. She would know, now, how old he was and her natural inclination would be to show greater respect to someone so much older than herself. Edwin waited to see what she would say next: whether she would back down or whether she would press ahead until the humiliation became too great for her and she would lapse into a sullen silence. He waited and it occurred to him that Matilda herself was having some difficulty deciding what to do. Several seconds passed before she spoke again.

'You're sixty-two?'

Edwin nodded and Matilda looked away. She was losing the battle, he thought; she wouldn't go on for much longer – it was not in her nature to pry.

'My doctor is sixty-two,' she said, rather too abruptly.

Again Edwin nodded but said nothing. He could see it now quite clearly in her expression – her embarrassment, her desire to break away and return to a more peaceful, less forced state.

'There's tea . . .' she suddenly said, and then stepped backwards, retreating down the hall before turning and walking back towards the open door at the far end.

Edwin followed her, the photographs still held loosely in his hand. Watching her the previous month, he had gained a sense of her secretiveness. She was someone, he had concluded, who liked to keep things hidden from view, who felt most comfortable when alone and unobserved. Of course, most people had a secret self but Matilda's – he had decided from the few hours he had spent in her company – was more keenly protected than most. She had remained aloof that day, allowing Jacob to take the lead while she maintained a watchful silence.

Edwin himself wasn't like that. He may have been once, but he had grown out of it long ago. As he'd aged, he'd found he had less desire to be guarded. Perhaps it was a result of spending so much time in his father's company – so many years safeguarding his father from pain, never raising the subject of his mother with him despite the questions that grew with him into adulthood. And once he reached maturity, he discovered his questions had settled like sediment, weighted down beneath layer upon layer of silence, until they became rock-like and he no longer possessed the tools to break them open. The fact that his father had never told him that his mother had not died the day she disappeared should have struck him as a betrayal – but he could not bring himself to feel deceived by his father. Instead, his compassion had increased for the man who raised him, and when he finally asked May to translate the article he had driven home afterwards in a state of despair. Not because he had discovered the truth about his mother at last but because he had acted disloyally; although his father was long since dead, Edwin felt he had betrayed him.

It had taken a few more years to reach the stage where he was now. The point where he could begin the search for the woman, who must, he thought, also be dead. Although only sixty-two, not really old by today's standards, he felt conscious of ageing, of 'living with age'. Foolish though it was, he felt death approaching. This may have been the reason why, waking one morning, he had felt a conscious desire to change. He had spent too long dithering. Lying in bed he made the resolution – weak at first but more powerful of late – to discover the missing pieces of his life, to gather himself together. He had woken that day with the desire to feel complete.

I asked Matilda what she wanted to do with her life. I asked because it was a question I had never been able to answer myself – at least not since the age of nine or ten when I had given up my dream of becoming a bee-keeper. She said nothing. There was a silence between us, so, in order to make it easier, I asked, 'What are you good at?' She responded, more quickly than I had anticipated, 'Nothing.'

I felt embarrassed; I had pushed her too far and she wasn't willing to submit to my interrogation. We hadn't known each other long – it was the day I delivered her photographs and she informed me the wedding had been called off.

'What would you like to do?' I probed. I don't understand why I kept pushing her. I expect I was nervous; I was trying to be friendly, fill in the awkward pauses that punctuated the sips we took from our tea – I don't know. But the role I had created for myself was false. I was overbearing, like some old friend of the family who pretends to be concerned when, in fact, he is no more than a pompous bully. Yet if I annoyed or upset her she showed no sign of it. She appeared thoughtful, and then responded, 'I would like to make a documentary.' I maintained my pretence of family friend;

I'm surprised I didn't say, 'Come now, child, whatever do you mean? A documentary?' However, I simply nodded and remained silent for several minutes. Then my curiosity got the better of me and I asked, 'What sort of documentary do you want to make?' I waited, expecting no more than an 'I don't know' but her reply, when it came, was very definite. Without a trace of irony, she replied, 'I want to make a documentary about old people.'

FIVE

Edwin glanced across to his passenger. She was turned away from him, looking through the window on her side of the car. Dust was beginning to seep in: fine, dun-coloured powder that hung in the air and caught in the back of his throat. Edwin opened his mouth to ask her to close the window but something stopped him. He didn't want such a demand to be the first thing he said since leaving her house. He didn't want to become, once more, the domineering man he had been while drinking tea with her only half an hour earlier.

His eyes on the road, he tried to recall the moment when he had suggested that she accompany him to the sanatorium. He felt puzzled. Why had he invited her along? It didn't make sense and yet the suggestion, when he had made it, had seemed perfectly natural. But the more he thought about it, the more certain he was that nothing in their previous conversation had led up to this moment: the point that had her sitting next to him in his car. It didn't bother him – the fact that she was here, travelling beside him towards the old sanatorium where he spent the first twelve years of his life – but it puzzled him. He wasn't sure what had happened.

Since leaving her house they had not spoken. That was the strangest thing of all. That they could travel together and yet say nothing, make no small talk. Every time he thought he might disturb the silence between them and introduce some topic or other, he found himself lacking the ability to follow through. Either his mind would go blank or he would dismiss whatever it was he could say as being of no interest. His problem, as he saw it, was that he really had only two options: he could talk about things that were not particularly important – the weather, the view of the river from the car, the number of dead rabbits on the road – or he could go to the other extreme and tell her about his decision to revisit his past, to find out what had happened to his mother and his attempt to make sense of his life. For the life of him he could think of no middle ground: some area that was interesting, worthy of dialogue and yet did not broach the deeply personal. He was surprised to discover that he was beginning to feel downhearted. It was ludicrous – the whole situation was completely out of hand. Why should he, an adult man with many years' experience in making small talk to strangers, suddenly find himself so tongue-tied in the presence of this girl – a girl, moreover, who had turned twenty-two only three days before?

For the first time in many years he wished he had not given up smoking. This would have been the perfect time, he realised, to reach for a cigarette and light up. If nothing else, cigarettes had always enabled him to buy time. They had obscured so many uncomfortable lapses in conversations. In the old days, he remembered, smoking even lent his studio a bohemian, swinging charm. It must have been around the time the film *Blow-Up* played in Dunedin. His business had picked up for a while after that. Suddenly, being a photographer was fashionable. Even though he was no fashion photographer, his work was nevertheless linked to that glamorous world – a world that never truly existed in Dunedin. Young girls who had seen the film would enter his studio in groups of three or four, giggling with excitement as they requested pictures for their 'portfolio' – images they intended to send off to magazines throughout New Zealand and Australia – even Britain, so confident were they of being 'discovered'.

It was all part of a game, and for a year or two he had enjoyed playing it. His hair was longer back then; he had long sideburns, of course. He even remembered one of the outfits he wore. The deep purple trousers made of crimplene – or perhaps polyester – the white belt and shoes, the floral shirt in shades of mustard, pink and purple. He looked good. He was slim, yet not weedy – athletic, almost. Although he had been plagued since childhood with kidney problems, he still smoked a pack a day. He enjoyed smoking and even took a certain amount of pride in the act itself. He was, he realised now, image-conscious back then – why else would he hesitate in front of the changing-room mirror and glance at his reflection, raising his cigarette nonchalantly to his lips as he looked on?

Of course it was all show. He was far too scared of forming any attachments. Looking back, he could count on the fingers of one hand the number of girlfriends he'd had. Invariably, after a fairly short period, he would find himself withdrawing from their company, retreating to the controllable world of bachelorhood. The term 'commitment phobic', which he had read about in the women's magazines at May's fish and chip shop, didn't exist back then. His girlfriends called him selfish or cold – even cruel – but no one had heard of 'commitment phobic'. However, having read those articles, he knew now that he had, in fact, been just that.

He glanced once more in Matilda's direction and took in her profile. He'd noticed before that she had good posture – she walked and sat with a very straight back, something that young children did naturally but was not usually associated with young adults. He wondered if she had taken ballet lessons. Certainly, given her height and her frame, she had the perfect body for a dancer. She was also graceful – he'd made a note of the way she walked when he had followed her into the house earlier in the day. Yet, he remembered, her toes did not point outwards when she was standing. Once, years ago, he had had to photograph a class of young ballerinas: a Saturday class of girls aged eight to twelve. Without exception they had all stood heels together, toes out – the overall impression he'd had of the group was that they resembled some old-fashioned floral clock, the hands pointing to ten past ten. Even when they'd walked in their street clothes, the girls had maintained what was, to him, an affected gait. All tippy-toes and bow-legged.

But though Matilda was light on her feet, she didn't appear in the slightest bit self-conscious. In fact, if anything, the opposite was nearer the truth. She gave the impression of being somehow removed from herself. He recalled the way she had wandered off during the photography session at the vineyard. While Jacob had stood chatting to his former girlfriend, Matilda had been content to stand beneath the tall poplars, a world away from the fracas taking place. She had, he remembered, carried a video recorder. Was that related to her documentary-making ambitions? His curiosity aroused, he cleared his throat and asked, 'You said you wanted to make a documentary. Have you made any yet?'

Out of the corner of his eye he saw her jump – his voice must have startled her – but, turning towards him, she smiled and said, 'No. Well, yes . . . sort of. I tried to make one.'

Edwin nodded, hoping she would continue of her own accord so that he wouldn't have to press her for details. But, as the silence between them lengthened, he prompted, 'What was it about? An old person?'

She shook her head. 'No. I don't really know any old people . . . It was about a hedgehog that lived in my garden. I had this idea that I would make a "Year in the Life of a Hedgehog" documentary – I started it late last year when my father sent me a video camera as an engagement present.'

Edwin couldn't help but smile. It wasn't that he found the idea of making a hedgehog documentary ridiculous – not at all. He liked the idea very much, but more than that, it aroused in him a desire to encourage the girl; it endeared her to him. The idea of following a hedgehog through a year of its life had a quiet charm, something akin to *The Wind in the Willows*, or a similar story. He wanted to encourage her; she seemed in need of it. 'It sounds like an interesting project. How's it progressing?'

A pause followed, and then Matilda replied, 'It's not. Jacob backed over the hedgehog in his truck one night.'

Laughter erupted from Edwin – he couldn't help himself. Trying to gain control, he spluttered, 'I'm sorry, I'm sorry. I didn't mean to laugh.'

To his relief, however, Matilda's mouth also seemed to quiver slightly around the edges. She was close to smiling. Her lips fluttering, she said, 'It was my fault. I shouldn't have encouraged it – I'd been putting out food on the lawn and it must have been wandering over for its tea when Jacob hit it.' Her lips curled slightly, then she added, 'I should have stuck to old people. They have better road sense.' She smiled again, giving the impression that what she had just said amused her. Edwin smiled too, though his smile was somewhat more nervous than hers, he guessed.

They travelled for several minutes without speaking, images of the hedgehog documentary playing through Edwin's imagination. From time to time he would glance back in Matilda's direction but she was no longer smiling; rather, she had turned her attention back to the view passing her window.

'You haven't got your camera with you today, have you?' asked Edwin. He knew the answer before she even shook her head. Of course she didn't have it with her; he hadn't seen it, had he?

'No,' she frowned. 'I thought I should leave it behind.'

Edwin caught the note of disappointment in her voice and found himself feeling sorry for her. Perhaps her desire to make a documentary was stronger than he had imagined – or given her credit for. Maybe she was one of those people who felt a real need to create something. All credit to her, if that was the case. He hoped she would fulfil her ambition. In an attempt to lighten the mood, he said, 'I hope you didn't leave it behind because of me.'

He was taken aback to hear Matilda sigh, 'Well, I did leave it behind because of you.'

Although Edwin couldn't quite know what she meant, he detected a trace of regret in her voice.

'I usually take it everywhere,' she continued. 'Just in case . . .'

In case of what? Edwin wanted to know but instead he fell silent, guilty for his part in stifling her art.

After several minutes Matilda broke the silence, saying, 'I've never been along this road before.'

It seemed to Edwin that she was apologising and once more

he found himself feeling both disconcerted and guilty – though quite why, he wasn't sure. To cover his discomfort he replied, 'It's changed a lot in recent years – not that I've been back for a long time.' He saw her nod but she made no effort to continue any conversation. However, feeling a sudden desire to talk – perhaps in order to cocoon himself with words – he said, 'This used to be a mining community. It was because none of the miners ever got TB that they decided to build the sanatorium around here – they thought the air must be particularly healthy . . .' He trailed off, wondering if air could be called 'healthy' rather than clean or fresh but made no attempt to clarify his meaning. Instead he concentrated on the road and the tendrils of ochre dust that continued to filter through the air vents in the dashboard and Matilda's open window.

He found himself thinking about his childhood. Despite the fact that he was driving ever nearer to the place where he had started out in life, his memory of that time was sometimes so distant that it was as if it had been written on a blackboard and then wiped clean with a duster. Whitish smudges remained, the faint outlines of words, but nothing quite distinct enough to be read easily. He had been blackboard monitor, he remembered. It had been one of his proudest moments: the week he had been entrusted with cleaning the blackboard and banging clean the dusters. He recalled the chalk dust that filled the air as he brought the two dusters together, the vague unease – that he was polluting the air with his dust. So much emphasis had been placed on the air at the sanatorium. It had been encoded with both clinical and magical powers. Settled in their beds on long verandas, the patients had been exposed to fresh air, summer and winter. He had rarely entered the wards, but, walking by, he could clearly see the line of beds, the faces of the patients fixed on the empty space ahead of them, the breeze from outside ruffling their hair, catching the edge of their bedcovers, tugging at the hospital corners, which refused to budge, so expertly were they tucked under.

His mother had been one of those patients. He knew that much about her. She had begun her nursing studies but within six months had contracted TB and been admitted to the sanatorium. She had thought, when she arrived, that she would be cured within a few weeks but had remained as a patient for two years. Then gradually, eventually, she had regained her strength, by which time she had developed a bond with Edwin's father – a man eighteen years her senior.

Edwin scratched his head. He really knew so little about his mother. She had no story – no history; nothing beyond the fragments he had been able to share as a young child – before she disappeared.

'There's a bridge, too,' Edwin suddenly remarked. 'It's made of iron. Reasonably famous, I think – among bridge enthusiasts.'

He perceived a smile cross Matilda's mouth and relaxed.

'I like bridges,' she said.

Edwin nodded, then asked, 'Better than old people?'

'No,' replied Matilda, 'but better than hedgehogs.'

Not wishing the conversation to die away, Edwin said, 'There's a nice bridge at Ophir. Have you seen it?'

Matilda nodded but then retreated once more into silence. Already, despite having known her such a short time, Edwin had observed a pattern in her behaviour: she would, for the most part, sit quietly, watching or listening to the conversations around her; eventually she would make some remark of her own and then, without fail, draw back into herself as if embarrassed by how much she had said.

This time, however, Edwin didn't want her to withdraw into her own world. He was feeling increasingly anxious about the journey he was making and he wanted something – or someone – to distract him. He searched his thoughts for something to say but his mind went blank. He couldn't think of anything that might engage the girl, and the more he felt a need for her company the less willing his brain appeared to be to help. Aware that it was probably the wrong question, but feeling increasingly desperate, Edwin asked, 'Why do you like old people, anyway?'

As he expected, Matilda made no response. For a moment he allowed himself to hope that she had not heard him but after a few seconds she sighed and he knew, then, that she would not be answering his question. He was surprised, however, to hear her enquire, 'Did you like your parents?' So preoccupied had Edwin been in recent months with thoughts of his father and mother that he felt confused by her question. For some reason he imagined that he had already told her everything he knew about his mother: her death, her resurrection – as he referred to it in his mind, and his decision to track her down. It came as a jolt, therefore, to realise that Matilda knew nothing at all about his journey. In that moment he felt more puzzled than ever as to why she was with him, asking him questions about his relationship with his parents. What on earth was going through her mind?

'I loved my father very much. We were very close,' he eventually replied.

He expected his answer to be absorbed into the deep shadow of silence but instead he heard Matilda respond, 'I would like to have been close to my father.' She coughed, choking a little, and then continued, 'I'm not, though. He lives in China – with his partner and her family. She – his partner – is not my mother. I've never met her and I haven't seen him for ages – years.'

Her reply raised questions in Edwin's mind but the tone in her voice discouraged him. The subject, he guessed, was now closed. Returning to safe ground, he remarked, 'Of all the rivers I've crossed, I think the Clutha has the nicest bridges.' He began to list them: Balclutha, Beaumont, Alexandra, the red bridge at Clyde, the old bridge at Cromwell . . . only the bridge at Albert Town let them down. It was ugly, no question about it.

Matilda listened as he spoke, and when he finished she said, 'I used to want a house with a drawbridge.' And at that she turned away, facing the window once more and the tussocklands beyond.

Sometimes the patients would give concerts. They had so little to keep them occupied they would stage plays, musical recitals, poetry readings ... anything to take their minds off the long hours of inactivity forced upon them. The healthier ones were encouraged to work in the garden; they would grow enough vegetables to feed everyone – staff and patients. Others would work on the small farm or in the sheds, doing everything from blacksmithing to mechanical repairs. The sanatorium was largely self-sufficient, you see. The people who were too sick to garden or work simply stayed in bed. Month in, month out they remained in bed – never moving from one day to the next. It was terrible for them. They had so little in the way of life. Life was stagnant.

But the concerts! I remember the concerts. Lights would be strung across the patients' dining hall and draped along the eaves. We had our own hydro-electric scheme, our own electricity supply. I tell you, we lived in our own small world. The lights would go up – long rows of them snaking and dipping the length of the main building. Sometimes, in summer, the concerts would go on far into the night. In fact they weren't concerts as such, but dances. I was too young to take part but whenever there was a dance I would find my way back to the main building and I would stand outside and look in and watch the healthier men and women dancing together. So many of the patients were young – no more than twenty or thirty – and I would watch them moving, as if in slow motion, from one end of the community room to the other. They glided, travelling in loose circles around the room like ice skaters – like the ice skaters at Naseby.

At first I used to think I was the only one outside looking in, but then I would glimpse another figure standing by himself, his body obscured by the deep shadows of the trees. It was a man – I could see that straight away. He had his back turned to the hall and was looking out over the plains, the light from his pipe flaring every now and again as he smoked. It's hard for someone from the city to understand how black those nights could be: that the lights from the dance hall could be the only lights for miles around. The blackness was warm, soft, I thought – like velvet. That's how I always pictured it – velvet nights filled with the sound of music. And my father, a dark shadow, standing by himself looking out across the emptiness.

SIX

As Edwin walked from building to building he felt the gulf between them and his memory of the sanatorium widen. His image of the place had been so clear, so precise in its detail, and yet time and time again he took himself to a site he remembered only to find he had been mistaken. It was not the blacksmith's workshop that stood in the shade of the shelterbelt, as he remembered, but the slaughterhouse. The women's pavilion had exchanged places with the men's. These were such huge lapses in memory it seemed to Edwin that none of his recollections might be correct. As he wandered around the site he began to feel increasingly desolate: why was nothing as he remembered it? The emerald green lawn that had fronted his own house, the vibrancy of which had contrasted so markedly with the dull, sunburnt tussock slopes of the surrounding hillside, was now burnt and straw-like. Yet it was around here that he had stood beneath his sunflowers. He knew there had been sunflowers.

And not just sunflowers but roses, too. There had been an archway: an arch made by the man who worked alongside the blacksmith. Ted. Ted had made his mother and father a frame for their climbing roses and there had been a picnic the day it was placed in the garden at the foot of the path, by the gate. Edwin was sure of it. The arch, the brick gateposts, the concrete path and the bird-bath: there had been a bird-bath in the centre of the lawn. The blackbirds used to splash around in it – he could recall his mother laughing as she watched them, saying, 'Look, Edwin, they're washing before dinner.' It was a kind of a joke she had – that the birds would wash and then fly over to the vegetable garden and tug at the newly planted rows, tearing up whatever had just been sown. He remembered – he was sure he remembered – that his mother never made any attempt to discourage the birds. She didn't cover any of the fragile plants with netting but, rather, seemed to enjoy watching the result of her hard work being uprooted and discarded. It was almost as if she only ever planted vegetables so that she could watch them being destroyed by the birds.

He remembered now that he had once made her a scarecrow for her birthday. He had managed to persuade one of the women in the laundry to part with a threadbare nurse's uniform and he had turned it into a scarecrow. He had made the head out of sack and had stitched eyes and a mouth onto it. The rest of the sack had been cut into strips, which he had then carefully sewn on to the top of the scarecrow's head for hair. It had taken him a long time and the result was somewhat ghoulish. That white nurse's uniform, which reached almost to the ground, the head with the staring eyes, and loosely embroidered grinning lips. The hair that blew, wild tendrils, in the wind.

He had got up very early on the morning of his mother's birthday and gone to the garden by himself to 'plant' the scarecrow. It had been his secret: everyone had known he was up to something – he had been unable to hide his growing excitement – but no one had guessed exactly what he was doing. He remembered the way the scarecrow had wobbled about on its central stick as he carried it from the shed behind the house to the garden. It had been so top-heavy that he had found it difficult to walk and he'd kept tripping as he made his way to the lettuce bed. In his mind now he could visualise what he must have looked like: an image of a procession of the Ku Klux Klan came to mind. Of course he had no idea that was how he looked back then. It was one of his proudest moments: the first thing he had made entirely by himself for his mother. He had no memory at all of her response.

Glancing up from the patch of grass by his feet, Edwin had a sudden desire to find Matilda. No sooner had they arrived than they had parted, his vague intention to show her around the derelict buildings coming to nothing. Now, however, he felt a strong urge to find her. The past hour of exploration had left him feeling hollow. Rather than reconstructing his childhood in its entirety, he had found himself remembering only bits and pieces, insignificant events punctuated by gaping holes. He had the feeling that if Matilda was with him, he might be able to remember things more clearly. Acting as a tour guide showing a visitor a site of special interest, he might have been better equipped to describe the place in a logical, methodical manner.

But, he realised, he was still feeling somewhat ambivalent about what he wanted to remember. If that was the case, Matilda might provide a buffer between the present and his memories. That was it: he could be the type of guide one encounters in a historical village – someone who can describe every detail, fragment by fragment, while knowing nothing at all about what really went on.

Edwin looked around, suddenly annoyed by his apparent reluctance in this search for his mother. He had come here, he thought, to reignite his past, to rediscover his mother and the brief life they had spent together. Hadn't he spent years anticipating this moment? He had planned for this day ever since he asked May to translate that article in the magazine – a feature on the community at Franz Josef, the people who lived and worked there, supporting the tourist industry, making their mark on the land. His mother, it turned out, had been one of those people: one of the first women to guide visitors onto the glacier. His mother, a tour guide. Just as he now wished he could be, he thought bitterly.

He looked back towards the car, hoping to find Matilda, but she was nowhere in sight. He felt a flash of irritation. Why on earth had he dragged her up here in the first place? His past had nothing to do with her; she played no part in his story. He hardly knew her – she was a girl forty years his junior! What had he been thinking of? Deciding to return immediately to the car so he could drive them both back to Ranfurly, he began to hurry, stumbling over the tufts of grass and tussock underfoot. As he approached his car he saw a figure standing next to it. It was not Matilda's slight, angular form, but that of a middle-aged man, a man nearer his own age, dressed in brown trousers and a polar fleece jacket. Edwin hadn't expected to come across anyone else at the sanatorium, though now that he gave it more thought he realised some of the smaller buildings did not look entirely abandoned, and his own former home had also looked maintained.

The thought that he might have to explain his presence to someone irked him. Already he had made a mess of his visit and he felt little desire to linger now that he had made up his mind to leave.

He heard the man call, 'Hello!', waving his hand in greeting as he approached. 'Hello.'

Edwin hesitated, surprised by the note of welcome in the man's voice. He had expected the man to appear suspicious, maybe even hostile, at finding a stranger on the property.

'Are you looking for someone?' the man called, walking up to Edwin. 'Because I think I've found her . . .' He spoke in a quieter voice, pointing with his hand in the direction of the main building. 'She was asleep on one of the lounge chairs – gave me one heck of a fright. I thought she was a ghost!'

Later, as he replayed his response to the man's remark, Edwin realised how bizarre his behaviour must have seemed. He had been caught off guard, that was all. When the man – Richard – had said, 'I thought she was a ghost!' Edwin, too, had thought Richard had found a ghost. For a brief moment he had believed Richard was referring to his mother – not Matilda. He'd realised his mistake almost straight away, but there had still been a moment, however brief, when he had believed that his mother – or the ghost of his mother – was lounging on one of the low-slung deckchairs that used to line the pavilion's corridor. And he had thought she was waiting for him.

In fact, that wasn't what Richard had meant. The woman was Matilda. He had found her outside the building known as 'The Diet' – the kitchen and dining area – asleep on a modern-type chair, the type sold in any of the cheap outdoor furniture chains, not one of the original lounge chairs.

Edwin followed Richard into one of the smaller staff houses and there, sitting at the kitchen table, looking awkward, was Matilda.

'Here she is!' Richard's voice seemed unnaturally loud in the almost empty room.

Although it had been years since he had last stood in this kitchen, Edwin knew it well. It had belonged to the matron – the woman who had for several years fulfilled the role of surrogate mother for him. Her name was Ida – it was a joke among some of the younger, healthier male patients. 'Look out!' they'd laughed as she'd approached. 'It's Ida from Ida Valley!' In all other ways they'd treated her with a great deal of respect. She was their link, they knew, between the hospital and the outside world. It was Ida they would approach whenever they needed permission to leave the sanatorium for a day or weekend. The stronger patients knew they could rely on her to put their case forward; she would make an approach to the doctor – Edwin's father – on their behalf. Often the request would be turned down, but such was the level of respect for his father, no one complained. That was the thing back then, thought Edwin: people didn't complain. Not because they weren't unhappy – some of the men had been desperate to return to their homes and earn a living once more – but because there was such a sense of community, a belief in a common cause. Their attitude struck Edwin as somewhat old-fashioned now, but he remembered those patients and the feeling of goodwill and respect that existed between them and the staff.

Catching sight of Matilda, Edwin thought he could detect a hint of anxiety in her expression. He guessed that having found her, Richard would have tried to establish what she was doing at the sanatorium and he could imagine the effect his questions might have had: her awkwardness as she tried to explain what she was doing. It dawned on Edwin then that he ought to have told her about his childhood and his reason for visiting this place. But she hadn't asked. It was as if Matilda regarded a trip to a run-down sanatorium with a man she barely knew as the most natural thing in the world.

Edwin didn't know what to make of her.

PART TWO

matilda

ONE

Matilda had enjoyed being up at the sanatorium. She realised that although she had never been there before she had been aware of its existence. It consisted of a large group of buildings – over twenty buildings, she thought – and they must have been visible from the house back in Ranfurly. Now that she thought about it, she knew she had noticed them before but she had not bothered to ask anyone about them. She'd been too taken up with other things: first the wedding, and then the matter of returning the few gifts they had been given. She'd also had to sort through her and Jacob's household goods, deciding what was hers and what belonged to him. In the end she'd given him everything. She hadn't wanted to keep anything except the video camera. That was hers. She needed it in order to make her documentary. That was what she was going to do. Even if it turned out to be the worst documentary ever made.

The entire contents of the house – Jacob's house – were as good as gone. She hadn't known how to tell Edwin but she had already moved out when he arrived. She had just called by to sort out a few final things before returning to the motel where she had been staying. She hadn't felt particularly concerned about where she would go next: she had money, and besides, she was a hard worker – she would do anything. The piano had been worth more than she thought; even the furniture had fetched a reasonable price – being 'genuine art deco' it was quite sought after, apparently. She also had her savings. She'd been working full time for around four years and every week for as long as she could remember she had put money aside and spent as little as possible on herself. She'd created a special account long ago: an account she referred to as the 'When everything turns to shit account'. And everything had turned to shit.

She hadn't been surprised when Jacob called off the wedding – she had always thought he would. She didn't blame him. The only surprise was that it had taken him so long. He was such a good man – deep down – that he hadn't had the courage to leave her any earlier. He'd let things slide, probably out of guilt. She realised that her very presence in the house must have made him feel guilty; that for weeks or months he had known he couldn't go through with the marriage and yet he'd been unable to tell her. Instead, he'd spent every day feeling increasingly awkward because he had known something she hadn't, and he hadn't said anything for fear of hurting her.

Perhaps if she'd been a better person she would have ended it herself. It seemed sometimes that she was only testing him anyway. Seeing how long he would stick by her. It was a cruel thing to do to a twenty-three-year-old. Looking back she saw she should have put him out of his misery, but for once she had allowed herself to hope that her life could be normal, without drama. She'd hoped that the wedding would go ahead and that they would be happy together. Yet, if things hadn't worked out she wouldn't have fallen apart. It sounded ruthless but if marrying Jacob had turned out to be a disaster, she could have lived with the consequences. It wouldn't have killed her. In some ways that was what she had wanted: the chance to make the same stupid mistakes as everyone else and not be destroyed by them. And, although she didn't particularly care about fitting in, she did want to engage in a world where she could stumble without falling off the cliff.

However, it was Jacob who had left her. He was the one who called off the wedding and it was the right thing for him to do. She understood why he had done it. He was too young to take her on. He had his whole life ahead of him – and despite what her doctors and counsellors encouraged her to believe, she didn't. So he left her. And she respected him for it.

She hadn't expected to feel so lonely, though. In the weeks following the non-wedding she had slowly drained; she was like a cracked tank, her contents seeping onto the dry ground, where they turned to mud. Soft, oozing mud that eventually dried and turned to dust. It was only now – now that the house was sorted out and everything was in storage or sold – that her body had attained complete hollowness. She felt tired.

That was why she had stretched out on the lounge chair. She had wanted to rest. Her body seemed to have lost some – or all – of its strength and she'd needed just to sit down for a minute. It wasn't as if she felt worried about her future – after all, she'd already accepted that it was pretty much a done deal. No, she was tired. And pissed off that she'd left her video recorder behind. She should have brought it.

A year ago things would have been different. This time last year she hadn't even operated a video camera. She hadn't wanted to. The closest she'd got to viewing an image on one was glancing up at the security camera mounted above the entrance to her local bank branch. Looking up as she passed through the door, she was always aware of her figure on the screen, the suggestion that she might be a bank robber caught on film. The gift from her father had been a complete surprise. She barely knew him. Although he was practically remarried, and with a new family, she guessed he was the same as ever: rich and hard-working. She knew he had a nice apartment and servants in China but she'd never visited him. She knew, too, that he had been told about what happened to her. She had a get well card to prove it.

For a long time she'd left the camera in its polystyrene packaging. She hadn't seen the point of it at first. It was a strange gift under the circumstances. There was nothing in her life she wished to record. In fact, if anything, she would have been far more grateful for a machine that enabled her to forget.

But then she'd read the instructions and, after all the time and effort she'd put into doing that, she felt obliged to at least try out the camera. Unexpectedly, she had felt comfortable using it. It enabled her to focus on things outside her own thoughts and body. It enabled her to step outside herself. It was a very comforting tool. She liked it, grew attached to it, and now, whenever she was separated from it, she felt less sure of herself.

The idea of making a documentary had come later. To begin with it was more of a joke than anything else. After all, what did she know about documentaries? Nothing at all. However, in her mind that, too, represented a type of freedom. She liked the idea of 'nothing' – of knowing nothing, instead of too much. It was comforting.

She'd been thinking about the documentary she wanted to make when Richard had found her. He hadn't crept up on her but had startled her nevertheless. All he'd said was 'Hello' and she'd jumped a mile. He hadn't asked what she was doing but had told her that he didn't get many visitors and would she like to come and have a cup of tea. She had thought he seemed a bit creepy and had glanced around, hoping to see Edwin close by. Edwin was nowhere to be seen. The man had introduced himself as Richard. Richard from Christchurch – as if that was a title he carried about. Eyeing him a moment longer, she concluded that he wasn't so much dangerous looking as *religious* looking. His eyes, like those of other religious types, held her gaze just a little longer than was comfortable. She had the impression that she would not be able to shake them off – shake him off – until he felt he had captured her attention and told her what she needed to hear. There was a sense of stubborn superiority in this man, she thought. But she had gone with him anyway because she felt she had no choice.

Sitting at Richard's table she had listened as he told her his story of how he came to own the sanatorium. He'd been working for an airline – had been employed by them for twenty-seven years and then one day, with little warning, he'd learnt that there were to be lay-offs. He had been living in Christchurch with Jeffrey, his partner of thirteen years – a flight attendant on the international routes, like himself. They had had a comfortable life, the two of them.

Then, one day he'd been made redundant and Jeffrey had not. It hadn't mattered much at first, Richard said. Their Merivale townhouse needed renovating and, being at home during the day, he had overseen the project – directing the builder, organising the plumber, nagging the electrician.

And then, sighed Richard, he'd begun to get depressed. He couldn't understand what was happening at first; he'd never been depressed before – but he started to dwell on things. In particular, he found himself thinking about why he had been made redundant and Jeffrey had not. In retrospect, he said, he should have sought counselling – before the bitterness set in – but instead he would spend hours dwelling on how the airline had dumped him – a man with almost thirty years' experience – and kept Jeffrey. He could spend an entire day thinking about it. He had given the best part of his life to the company but had been discarded. Even now he felt a lump in his throat as he thought about how unfairly he had been treated.

Jeffrey had been supportive at first. He said he understood what Richard was going through. That it was grief. Then, after a few months, he grew less patient. 'What did it really matter?' he'd ask. 'You were planning to retire in a few years anyway. I'd love to be on permanent vacation. Enjoy yourself.'

Eventually, after almost a year, Jeffrey demanded that Richard move on and find closure. Three months later Jeffrey had begun to invite a colleague around for brunch on Sundays. His name was Hayden; he was Jeffrey's age, more or less. He made Jeffrey laugh.

It was about this time, continued Richard, that he saw a small notice in the paper. The sanatorium – all twenty-six buildings – was up for tender. Seeing that notice had had a remarkable effect on him. The thing was, he explained, he had once spent eight months living in these buildings. Once they'd found a way to treat TB, he told Matilda, there had been no reason to maintain a sanatorium so it had been turned into a kind of borstal: a home for problem boys. And because as a teenager he had been

—86—

caught several times in the arms of other boys – boys who shared his 'sickness and perversities' – he had been marked out as a potential criminal. No, not a 'potential' criminal but a criminal, plain and simple. A deviant. A pervert. And, despite hating every single second of every single day of those eight months, he had found that once he left, he missed the place. For better or worse, it had been his home.

So he put in a tender and it was accepted. He then sold his share of the townhouse to Jeffrey, left him – and Hayden – in Merivale, and withdrew. 'So, that's what I'm doing here,' he concluded. He looked at Matilda as if trying to penetrate her thoughts, then added, 'Now it's your turn. What are you doing here?'

It was at that point that it dawned on Matilda that she didn't know.

Back in Banana in Queensland, where I spent most of my school years, we grew sorghum. Coming from New Zealand I'd imagined that sorghum must be the most exotic plant in the world. I remember flying into Rockhampton that first time with my mother, Charlotte, and asking her about it. In my head I had pictured something tropical: fuchsia pink or blood red, large, open star-shaped flowers like waterlilies, growing out on long stems, their heads bobbing in the breeze. I couldn't wait to see what it really looked like: I was so certain it was going to be spectacular. I must have been around nine or ten years old. No one had told me that sorghum was going to be beautiful – it was something I'd made up all by myself.

It seemed to take ages to drive from Rockhampton to Banana. You might as well know that I was expecting to see a house in the jungle surrounded by bananas and clumps of bamboo and jungle animals. There would be lizards: big ones, giant ones – as big as me. I'd been drawing pictures of the place for weeks – ever since my father had told me my mother wanted me back. I hadn't seen her for months. I'd never met her new husband, Sandy.

I realise now that my mother must have been feeling very tense. In the few hours since meeting me at Brisbane and travelling with me up north, she hadn't really known what to do with me. She was always stressed because of me. I think she felt bad about how she had left me behind. As a result of her guilt, she would get frustrated and then impatient and angry. I don't know. I only know I broke her heart.

As we got closer to town, my mother suddenly erupted, 'Just shut up, will you? It's called Banana after a bullock. It was a huge bull thing, a browny-yellowy coloured cow. It was the most famous thing about the place. No one names a town after a banana. God, you're stupid.'

I'd forgotten that that was how my mother talked to me. Well, maybe I hadn't. I mean, if I'd really forgotten I might have felt more excited about seeing her than the sorghum.

TWO

Sitting beside Edwin during the drive back to town, Matilda felt cheerful. Though experience had taught her there didn't have to be a reason for her sense of well-being, she hoped, nevertheless, that in this particular instance the events of the afternoon might have some bearing on the way she now felt. She hoped she wasn't simply experiencing another of her fairly frequent though unpredictable mood swings. Looking back on her visit to the sanatorium, she realised she had enjoyed herself. Moreover, the day had been restful, a respite from the weeks of stress she had experienced since breaking up with Jacob. The sense of unease she had carried within her for so long had, for the moment at least, diminished and she was, without doubt, happy. It was such an unfamiliar feeling that she almost distrusted it. It was absurd, however, to be frightened by happiness. You're going mad, she told herself. Just be happy for once. Enjoy it. Stop worrying.

Earlier in the day she had felt anything but light-hearted. Sitting at Richard's table, she'd practically drifted off to sleep as he rambled on about himself. She had been aware of his story – his description of how he came to be living at the sanatorium – but all the time her thoughts had been elsewhere. They'd meandered through a canyon of topics: from Edwin and her hope that he would soon materialise and rescue her from Richard's ongoing saga, to memories of Jacob and their life together. She recalled the day of their wedding photographs, and her brief introduction to Jennifer.

For no particular reason it was the memory of Jennifer that occupied her thoughts the longest. Once they had finished having their photographs taken, the two groups had met up in the tasting lounge and spent the rest of the afternoon sitting around, drinking and talking. It had, Matilda recalled, been a somewhat dull ending to an already taxing day. The hours had dragged on, Jacob and Jennifer happily chatting away while Jennifer's husband-to-be, Luke, and his friends became increasingly drunk and sullen. They had been completely uninterested in Matilda – unable to initiate any conversation and reluctant to respond to anything she said. After several feeble attempts both Luke and Matilda had given up; he had turned back to his friends, leaving Matilda isolated and uncomfortable. In order to hide her discomfort she had focused all her attention on her video recorder, fiddling with its controls as she aimlessly studied its component parts.

From time to time Jennifer had remembered that Matilda was seated next to her and had tossed a question in her direction. Yet it was immediately clear that Jennifer was not interested in hearing her reply. Rather, she wanted to answer each question herself. As if hitting a ball against a wall, Jennifer utilised a back-and-forth volley of questions and answers to talk about herself, which was both bizarre and exhausting for anyone listening. Jennifer thus directed the conversation and revealed facts about herself while maintaining the appearance of being interested in the people around her. In this respect she was very similar to Richard, and to the girls Matilda had boarded with at high school in Gladstone, Queensland.

Like Jennifer, Richard had slipped easily into the dual role of quizmaster and contestant. He'd made small talk at first, attempting to engage Matilda in conversation about the weather, the previous summer and the onset of darker evenings. He'd asked her questions about herself: what she did for a living, where she lived. And while he had listened and nodded encouragingly as she struggled to describe herself, she could sense his impatience and his growing urge to interrupt, to tell her more about himself.

He'd probably expected her to ask him something – that was the normal procedure, after all – but in all honesty she could think of nothing she wanted to know. It wasn't that his story was not interesting – though she had her doubts – but rather that she didn't know how to go about entering what might be a private world. Although she knew he wanted to talk, she couldn't bring herself to ask the necessary probing, prying questions to set him on his journey. So eventually he had simply gone ahead without her. At the finish, satisfied, he had sat back and asked how she came to be sitting outside one of his buildings. It was a simple question – one that anyone in his position would have asked – and yet Matilda hadn't known the answer.

Visiting the sanatorium was Edwin's story, not hers. She had simply tagged along, and now, without Edwin at her side, she felt awkward and exposed. She longed for him to appear and take over so that she might fade into the background and return to the solitude she had enjoyed earlier in the day, the peacefulness of resting in a chair listening to nothing more than the wind passing through the trees and the trilling of the grey warblers above her.

She had felt pounded by all Richard's questions. As she'd struggled to think of something to say, she'd found herself withdrawing until, in the end, when he'd asked her to tell him about Edwin, she'd responded, 'I can't.'

Not satisfied with her response, Richard had attempted to prompt her, asking, 'Come on! You're spending the day with him. You must know something about him. At least tell me what you like about him?'

Feeling increasingly pressured, Matilda had been forced to respond, blurting out the first thing that came into her head. 'I like him because he doesn't ask questions. He respects my privacy.'

Eventually Richard had given up on her. She made such a poor audience that he felt obliged to search out another. He had gone looking for Edwin, returning ten minutes later looking refreshed and relieved.

Seeing Richard's smiling face, Matilda had realised how rude she must have been. She hadn't meant to appear so off-hand. Her reply had been intended to provide space, time out from Richard and his probing. There was, however, some truth in the remark. Edwin didn't ask questions. He wasn't like either Richard or Jennifer; in fact, he was different from most people she had met. He respected her privacy but, more than that, he seemed content to let things – information, events, even lives – unfold at an unforced pace. He gave her time. Edwin was the type of person who stood back and made room for disclosure. So often, it seemed to Matilda, people simply grabbed all information, sucking it up regardless of whether or not it was needed. She was often amazed at how greedy people were. Everyone, it seemed, wanted to know everything about everyone else *now*, this instant – never standing back and waiting for the proper place and time. People took short-cuts: finding out everything about a person without first going to the trouble of learning anything about them. It was something she got more worked up about than most. She had lived in a small town, after all. She knew how people talked.

What she would also have liked to say to Richard was: 'Because Edwin doesn't talk about himself all the time. He doesn't *need* to be noticed the way everyone else does. That's why I like him.' But she hadn't said it. There was no point; Richard wouldn't have understood. She wouldn't have made sense. She should have just told the truth: that she hardly knew Edwin, and she hadn't even thought about whether she liked him or not.

They had been driving almost twenty minutes when a thought suddenly entered Matilda's mind. Turning to Edwin she asked, 'If you were thinking of going to a film would you need to know how long it was and what it was going to be about before you went in, or could you just go and see it and find out that way?'

It was several seconds before Edwin answered. 'I don't go to many films. I'm not really a cinema person.'

Matilda nodded. 'Me neither.'

'But,' continued Edwin, 'if I was to go to a film I wouldn't want to know the plot. Mind you, I would like to have some idea of what the film was about . . . I don't want to spend ten dollars on some action or fantasy film, for instance.'

Matilda laughed. 'Ten dollars! It's more like fifteen.'

It was Edwin's turn to smile. 'Don't they have pensioner rates any more?'

Matilda frowned, 'You're not a pensioner yet. You're too young.'

She felt safe, somewhat disengaged; she began to wonder why she had lied to Edwin about the hedgehog. She remembered, quite clearly, 'the night of the hedgehog's death'. It had happened the night Jacob called off the wedding. Even though she had half expected it, his announcement had thrown her off balance and she had felt an immense urge to get out of the house, to escape from him as quickly as possible.

She had wanted to feel some air on her face but as she'd biked down the concrete path she'd felt a bump beneath her wheel and there, behind her bike, lying in shadow, was the hedgehog, flattened but alive, its guts oozing across the path. It had made her sick to the pit of her stomach but she had forced herself to stamp on the hedgehog's head, and she had heard a squelch as her boot struck hard against the path, flattening the creature's skull. She remembered being so upset that for several hours she had not been able to think of anything else. All thoughts of Jacob and the wedding evaporated. Like some ten-year-old in a film she had climbed back on her bike and pedalled away as fast as she could, into the night. And she would have kept on biking and biking had she not had a slow puncture – out on this very road. The same road she had denied ever having travelled along only that morning.

She turned to Edwin, determined to tell him the truth about the hedgehog, but, noting his expression, she hesitated. He was frowning, deep in thought. Although she had no idea what he was thinking about, he looked too serious to be interrupted with a story about a hedgehog. Discreetly, Matilda glanced at him again and realised that his expression was like the one he had worn an hour or so ago, while listening to Richard. Perhaps it was just her imagination but there had been a few occasions during the afternoon when Edwin had looked agitated, as if he was unsure whether or not he wanted to hear what Richard was saying. Yet at other times Edwin himself had talked easily, describing his childhood at the sanatorium. Matilda had found his descriptions of the place fascinating. There was one thing, however, that struck her as odd – the fact that although he talked openly about his father, spoke of him with an obvious warmth and fondness, he had made no mention of his mother. Though he had chatted with Richard for more than half an hour, and had answered many of Richard's infuriating questions, he had remained silent on the subject of his mother. It was almost as if she had never existed.

One other aspect of the visit had caught Matilda's attention. At one point Richard had mentioned that a few years earlier two very old women had visited the sanatorium. It had turned out they had lived there many years before, back in the forties or fifties. Richard wasn't sure of the exact dates but, he guessed that the women were both in their seventies or eighties. He paused for a moment, then added that despite their age they had looked healthy, the way people who live in the country so often appear: strong despite their years.

Of the two women, only one had talked. The other had remained silent throughout much of the afternoon and he had thought at first that she was slightly senile – unable to follow the conversation. Eventually, however, he had changed his mind, concluding that she was probably just hard of hearing. From time to time the more talkative woman would address her as if seeking confirmation of some fact or other, saying, 'Isn't that right, Jess?'

and the woman, Jess, would nod her head but otherwise maintain her silence. To be perfectly frank, he had found the silent
woman's behaviour slightly disconcerting. In fact the feeling was
stronger than that – she made him feel uncomfortable. It was as
if, he explained, there was a shadow about her, an aura of sadness
– as if she had experienced some terrible loss or tragedy in her
life. He had laughed then, explaining that in his former life he
had sometimes consulted a spiritualist and from her had learnt
about auras and chakras and such. He believed in that type of
thing, he said, without offering any further explanation.

Matilda had been looking at Edwin when Richard mentioned
the name Jess and had been surprised to see him visibly flinch.
It had been barely discernible but it had been no less powerful
for that. It was a gesture she recognised because it had been one
she had made herself on the day her doctor had called, asking
her to return to his surgery because he had something to tell her
– information he could not give over the phone.

As Edwin had sat quietly, Richard had continued to natter,
explaining how as a flight attendant working in first class he had
acquired the skill of remembering names. By concentrating on
some visual feature – a facial mark or a gesture – he was able to
make connections between a face and a name. For example, Jess,
the silent woman, had a strange scar just above her lip. It gave
her face a slightly lopsided look, which reminded him of a farm
dog his uncle once owned. The dog's name, curiously, was Tess
– hence the connection: lopsided grin . . . Tess . . . Jess. Not that
Jess looked like a dog, he laughed, but that was how his method
worked – visual connections. The other woman had no facial
marks but she did have lively eyes: they were green – ocean
green. Her name, he finished, was Violet.

Matilda had felt disturbed by Edwin's expression, the way he was simply staring into space. He reminded her of someone who, for whatever reason, could no longer make sense of his surroundings. She knew that look, she *knew* it, and although she had no idea what had caused it, she felt her heart go out to him. Yet, despite recognising his isolation, she had said nothing. Instead she had taken the only action that seemed to her – at that moment – to be respectful: turning away from him, allowing him the privacy he needed. But his expression had stayed with her. She had seen that something was wrong, that Richard's conversation had set something – she didn't know what – in motion. She had listened more carefully from that point on, had been aware of Richard saying, boasting almost, that he even remembered Violet's surname: it was Gray – which was amusing, didn't they agree? Neither Edwin nor Matilda had responded and the room had fallen silent.

No one had spoken for several seconds. Richard had stood up and gone to look through the window, plucking at his jersey – some minute balls of lint – as he gazed out across the garden. After some time Matilda heard Edwin sigh and then listened as he asked: 'The other woman's name – Jess – can you remember her surname?'

Richard had shaken his head. 'No, I don't know her name. I'm not sure I heard it . . .' Then, smiling, he had added, 'Unless I've simply forgotten it.' There was something triumphant in his tone, as if he was pleased with himself for being able to forget a name. He gave the impression that he had been released from some terrible bind, a talent that no longer gave him pleasure but had nevertheless maintained its hold over him for years and years.

Still picking at the pieces of fluff on his jersey, he went on.

'I have Violet's address somewhere. She told me she had some cartons of photographs of the sanatorium and invited me to look at them at her home in Alexandra.' He sighed, too dramatically, thought Matilda, before adding, 'Of course, I've been so busy with this place that I haven't had time.' His voice trailed off and he wandered over to the cork board hanging on the wall next to the telephone. He flicked through the scraps of paper layered deep on its surface. 'Her address is here somewhere . . .' Finding the piece he was looking for, he copied the address onto a yellow post-it note, which he passed to Edwin. 'Violet was a good-looking woman. Strong. Do you remember her?'

Edwin, Matilda recalled, had shaken his head. He said little after that but had sat very quietly, his palms pressed against his thighs, glancing occasionally towards the window as if expecting someone to walk by. Eventually, after a period of silence, he sighed and carefully folded the post-it note into quarters before tucking it carefully into his trouser pocket. Then he had shrugged his shoulders and smiled, looking embarrassed. 'Sorry,' he said, though to whom he was speaking, Matilda could not tell.

It was because Edwin had remained so downcast that Matilda had spoken to him on the journey back to Ranfurly about films. She had felt she ought to do something to lift the mood, and not being confident when it came to making small talk, she had grasped at the first thing that had entered her head: movies. Now, however, she felt uncomfortable. She didn't know why but she had the impression that she had let him down, that she had not done anything to help. She definitely had the feeling he needed help.

Retreating into herself, she began to replay the conversation that had taken place at Richard's, looking for clues that might explain Edwin's mood. Before Edwin had fallen silent, she had felt drawn into his stories of sanatorium life, willing them to continue so that she could visualise more clearly the life he had experienced. For a while she had even considered that the sanatorium itself might make a good subject for her documentary. But as Edwin spoke, it dawned on her that the thing that continued to hold her attention was not the sanatorium but Edwin himself. Although he wasn't particularly old – at least not in the way she defined old age – he appeared almost to belong to a previous age. A quiet age, one she wished she had known. She'd have liked to have had a childhood like his: one that simply unfolded day by day rather than collapsing into a frightening mess, as her own childhood had. Compared to hers, his life had been calm. He was lucky.

The reason Matilda liked old people was simple: it was because they were still alive, because they had survived. She sometimes wondered if old people understood or appreciated that – or even thought about it. She hoped they did. She wanted to think that every now and again an old person would take a step back from their everyday life in order to murmur appreciatively, 'At least I'm still here.' To Matilda, that was one of the few things worth saying.

There had been a time, not so long ago, when Matilda had believed she didn't deserve to live. Few people knew of that time in her life – her mother, her younger half-brother . . . her stepfather. Not her real father. He belonged only to the years of her early childhood, when she lived in Auckland.

Like everyone else in Auckland she had been aware of his presence. He had a high media profile, appearing on television, in magazines and at charity events. For most of her childhood it seemed to Matilda that the only place he rarely showed his face was at home. He was a very successful businessman and, as such, was less a physical presence in her life than a financial one. He paid for things.

They had lived on the North Shore. Her father and mother were already part of the establishment when she was born. Of course they hadn't always been so wealthy. Matilda had discovered that her parents had met in a bar in London. Her mother had been a waitress, her father a customer. They had quickly established a connection based on an identification of their accents: his was New Zealand, hers Australian. Amid all the noise and strangeness of the city, it had been enough to bring them together.

Returning to New Zealand, Matilda's father was well liked by everyone – except, it turned out, her mother. Settling down in an eight-bedroom home in Takapuna, Charlotte, Matilda's mother, had quickly discovered that she had no power over her husband, nor his schedules, meetings or gala events. She felt diminished and, because of that, took to hiring staff. Not because she needed help around the home but because the people she hired were, by definition, beneath her and she could tell them what to do. They were employed to notice her. But even that plan failed. The staff didn't notice her; she was too timid, too respectful. She hardened herself; trained herself to be less reasonable, more critical. She learnt that the only way she could gain any sense of self was by reminding her employees that she was in charge. Her behaviour shamed her; she wondered what had happened to her, how she could have become unrecognisable, even to herself.

In a last attempt to improve herself, to become a better, more interesting person, she decided one day to begin an art collection.

She had no real interest in art but had noticed that among the wives of her husband's associates, art played a major part in the conversation. Visiting the pristine concrete houses maintained by the wives she was able to learn – and recognise – the names of the artists held in their collections. At first she was surprised that most appeared to collect only the works of a few artists – there was little or no variation in the art work displayed on the walls of their personal galleries. However, after a while she understood that the most important part of collecting was the fact that art was the means to attaining status: acquiring the right painting allowed her to enter a new class, and although it was a group with a strong hierarchy (and she would never get off the bottom rung) she was glad, nevertheless, to be a member.

Then one morning, as she lay in bed gazing at her latest purchase – a work she liked, though she couldn't say why – Charlotte realised that in all the time she had been collecting, she had never spoken to an artist. At first she thought she must be mistaken – at one of the many openings she had attended she must have been introduced to at least one artist – but the more she searched her memory, the more certain she was that she had never talked to any painter about their work, or why they painted. And despite the sun, the stream of light that poured into her room, she had felt a sudden chill. She knew, without doubt, that she had failed.

And that was the mother Matilda had first become aware of; that was the mother she knew.

She pictured her mother as a person who had forgotten how to live. She recalled that her mother used to talk about a trip to Vienna, a visit to the hairdresser or an appointment with the school principal in such a way that it appeared she was unable to distinguish between them. Her mother's behaviour confused her – she didn't understand. She would look and look and look at her mother and she appeared like any other adult woman. There was nothing missing from her face or her body, but Matilda could not make her mother *work*. She didn't understand what had happened to her mother, but once she had been watching her father work on his computer when it had crashed. Hearing her father explain the problem – his description of how the computer had frozen; that all the information was still there but unobtainable – made Matilda think of her mother. She concluded that, like her father's computer, her mother had simply crashed.

Matilda had hoped her father would be able to fix her mother. She willed him not to go away on business trips. Whenever he was home she would push him towards her mother in the hope that his body, his presence, would make things better. She would watch, barely able to breathe, as her father kissed her mother and she would wait for her to return his embrace. And time and time again, nothing would happen. Her mother's eyes would flicker in recognition but she would say little beyond reciting some schedule of activities that was lined up for the forthcoming week – a charity event at the gallery, cocktails at the museum, dinner with the Pearsons, barbecue at the yacht club . . . As far as Matilda could tell, her mother didn't engage in any of these events; she attended them but her experience was such that they might just as well have been titles listed on a programme rather than anything real.

What Matilda did not know was that her mother was not, as she imagined, past caring. The fact was, her mother cared deeply. The greater her husband's success, the more pronounced her own sense of failure. And of all her failures, Matilda was her greatest. Matilda was the one thing in the whole world Charlotte wanted to care about and yet so entrenched was her behaviour, her reliance on the barrier erected between herself and those around her, that Charlotte didn't know how to approach her daughter. She didn't know what to say to her. Try as she might, she had nothing to talk about.

Looking at Matilda, Charlotte saw a mirror reflecting all the things she had done wrong. This caused her so much pain that she decided the only way she could make things better was by finding other people to do the job she was so clearly unable to perform. She didn't want to risk hurting her daughter any more than she already had. So once again she hired help: a nanny. And so the wheel of her own defeat began to turn again – but this time, unlike before, Matilda was riding beside her.

Then, one day, when Matilda was about six, her mother left. It wasn't until she was an adult that Matilda understood what had happened: that her mother was depressed; that she had been overcome by loneliness; that she had been experiencing the isolation of being married to a man who was always too busy, too tired or too preoccupied to maintain a relationship. At the time of her mother's departure Matilda had no idea of what had happened. Her father had appeared one day, lifted her high in the air and said, 'And now we can have some fun!' He'd hugged her and added, 'While the cat's away, the mice will play!' and then disappeared into his office, reappearing once or twice each day to lift her up and laugh: 'Now we'll have some fun!'

Matilda spent most of the following week playing outside, floating leaves on the pond – the 'infinity pool' – in the garden. Now that her mother was gone she didn't have to worry that the leaves would turn brown and sink to the bottom of the pool.

Part of the 'fun' that her father had talked about was not having to worry any more. The other part of her father's fun was his departure to Britain. Matilda didn't mind. On the few occasions she had spent time with him she had felt lost for words. Despite her father's proximity during the past week, she hadn't known what to say to him. Going for a walk together, she discovered that although she could answer any of his questions, she couldn't proceed further than that – she couldn't make conversation with him. The few times she had tried she had been struck by the impression that her father found her boring. Although he never interrupted her, he always seemed to be only half listening to whatever it was she was saying, his eyes wandering from her to his surroundings to his watch and back to her. She didn't know how to hold his attention so she did the only thing she could do: she retreated into silence.

The morning before her father left, an older woman arrived to stay. She was a stranger to Matilda, someone her father or his secretary had found. Matilda couldn't imagine that this stranger would be interested in her life so it came as a surprise to discover that the opposite was true. The stranger, it turned out, was perceptive. Without making a fuss, she quickly established herself as a presence in Matilda's life. At first Matilda didn't understand what was going on. She would be engrossed in one of her many projects only to stop, look up and see the stranger watching her. For one of the first times in her life, Matilda was aware of making eye contact with an adult. It was a remarkable experience, one she would never forget: the simple fact of being seen.

It was the stranger who took the time to explain to her that her mother had not simply walked out but was sick – not physically but mentally; that the thoughts in her mother's head were so powerful they could cause pain but Matilda was not to worry because her mother would get better. In a few weeks' time everything would return to normal; her mother would come home. 'In the meantime,' the stranger said, 'you are not to worry. This is a matter for grown-ups, not children. This is not something you have to be scared about or try to fix, so you're not to worry about your mum – or anything else, for that matter. I'm here now and I'm going to take care of everything. I'm going to look after you.' Then, giving Matilda a hug, the stranger had added, 'That's what I'm paid for.'

I wanted to make Edwin laugh. I don't know very many funny stories but I do know one – it's the story of how I met Jacob. I was working on a charter boat, up north on the Whitsunday Islands. The vessel, the *Sail-Easy*, was a luxury craft with a glass bottom. Passengers paid to spend a day cruising over the reef while enjoying the fine wine and light meals served by its friendly, helpful crew. Me, in other words. Although the work itself was easy, I found it tiring. I wasn't well at the time. In fact I was pretty sick.

We used to get a lot of wedding parties. In Australia weddings are big business – but then I guess it's the same here. On this particular day there were sixty people on board, the maximum number we could carry. It was a beautiful day, not a breath of wind and just a slow, gentle swell. The reef appeared to glow and flash, so bright were the coral and the small fish that swam about. It was so beautiful. I wish I'd learnt to use my video camera back then so I could have filmed it. Nevertheless, I felt sick. I was feeling so ill that I began to wonder if the side-effects from the drugs I was taking might be worse than the sickness itself. At least I could make sense of my disease. The drugs were another matter. Anyway, all I wanted to do that day was lie down and sleep or, better still, die for a couple of hours – until the party was over. It was that kind of day.

At one point I was standing in a corner of the lounge, resting for a moment, when I became aware of a commotion outside. I glanced through the window and I could see this naked guy larking about in the sea. He looked happy: treading water, duck-diving and waving to the passengers. Suddenly I saw him dive down and disappear from view, then a few seconds later I heard a cry of disgust from one of the guests, a woman in the lounge not far from me. She was staring at the window on the bottom of the boat so I went over for a look and there, with his arse pressed hard against the glass, his hands and arms sculling frantically and bubbles pouring from his nose, was the guy I'd just seen. It was really odd. Pressed against the glass, his bum looked like some giant sea sponge: it was kind of pale and mottled – and huge. He didn't hang around for long but in the short time he was there I half expected to see little fish swimming in and out of his crack. His bum really looked like something from the reef.

Anyway, he disappeared after a few seconds and from the noise outside I guessed he had surfaced once more. I heard the skipper's voice yelling at him to return immediately to the boat, but he didn't because a short while later he was back again, his bottom up against the glass just like before, but this time his hands were fluttering like the fins of a small fish – like that clown fish, Nemo – in his attempt to stay pressed against the pane. The next thing I knew he rolled over and pressed his stomach and penis up against the glass. That was really weird – his penis looked so strange, what with his testicles and everything: kind of half anemone and half hairy, whiskery sea slug . . . I don't know. It was like something you would expect to see on the reef, but at the same time it was like nothing at all – it was just bizarre. I couldn't take my eyes off it, it was so weird.

From beside me I heard the bride say to her new husband, 'Dave, I so don't need this today. I've got a lot on my plate, you know?' Dave just grunted, which made the bride even angrier, so she began to yell, 'Why did you invite him anyway? You don't have to invite every relative in the phone book! You're meant to be selective!'

I didn't see what happened next because at that moment I felt a wave of nausea run through me and it was all I could do to yank the bottle of champagne from the ice bucket I was holding before vomiting.

I wasn't fired – I was too hard a worker for that. Instead, I was given the rest of the day off and I found myself on an inflatable dinghy being driven to shore. The bum guy – Jacob – was in the boat with me. Neither of us spoke, though Steve, the crew member driving the boat, kept saying, 'You're a disgrace, mate. This isn't some cheap, budget do – this is a class wedding. Jesus, mate, the bride's granny was there! You might have spared a thought for her before you started flashing your dick around. Shit, mate, you should be fed to the sharks.'

I was too sick to say anything. It took all my strength just to get rid of the image of his privates flattened against the glass. We got dumped on the beach and then Steve headed back to the boat. I can remember the two of us sitting at the water's edge, side by side, both too wasted to move. I don't even know who spoke first.

THREE

With only a few kilometres to go before they were back in Ranfurly, Matilda's earlier sense of well-being gave way to panic. Aware that she would soon be dropped off, in town, she had the overwhelming feeling she was about to lose Edwin. For some reason that mattered to her. She was sure there was something going on that she hadn't yet fathomed and, despite her strong feelings about an individual's right to privacy, she felt a strong urge to ask questions. But, at a loss as to where to begin, she simply blurted out the first thing that came into her head: a question that immediately made her cringe, so blunt did it sound on her lips. 'Why didn't you mention your mother today? You didn't say anything about her.'

The question must have caught Edwin off guard because he jumped at the sound of her voice, the wheel of the car jerking to the left momentarily before he regained his composure. Still staring straight ahead, he asked, 'What do you mean?'

Matilda was mortified. Asking the question was bad enough but having to explain it was even worse. Not only had she invaded his space but she was having a good rummage around as well. Although it made little sense, and only served to increase her embarrassment once the words were uttered, she felt obliged to disclose some secret about herself in return. Thus, instead of following up her initial question with a second, she suddenly confessed, 'I killed the hedgehog, not Jacob.' On seeing the confused look on Edwin's face, she immediately felt even more stupid. Quickly she added, 'Thank you for taking me with you today. It made me feel better.' Then she fell silent. Glancing across to Edwin, she sensed that his frown had deepened and she felt ashamed. He must think she was either mad or thick – or both. There was nothing she could do now to save the situation. She had lost him.

Feeling dejected and sick with herself, Matilda kept her eyes on the road ahead, murmuring, 'You can drop me here,' as they entered the main street. It was all the same to her, where he left her – it didn't really matter. She would walk. She didn't register Edwin's lack of response to what she had said about the hedgehog or her day out, nor did she pay much attention when he asked, 'Is there a motel around here?' Mechanically, she pointed down the street. 'Down that way, you'll see it.' And then she was out of the car, closing the door and stepping away from it, her body gathering distance from Edwin. She could see his lips moving but she couldn't hear what he said. She hesitated for a second and made as if to step back towards the car but just as she did, the car jolted forward and Edwin drove away.

Matilda watched as he turned the corner, and felt overcome by helplessness and disappointment. It was all she could do not to cry out, such was the force of her emotion. Why, she asked herself, had she behaved like such an idiot? What was wrong with her? She couldn't make sense of her behaviour, and in her state of disbelief and rage she found herself looking around as if searching for a weapon, something she could use against herself – a baton or a stick, or even a bottle – so desperately did she want to feel the pain of her frustration. If there was just something she could run at – a brick wall would do – she could knock some sense into her thick skull. She glanced around and realised immediately that she was surrounded by walls – of all kinds. She was standing on the main street of a small town – of course there were walls: shop-fronts, buildings, houses . . . walls everywhere. An entire street of them. She smiled bitterly, knowing that she would run at none of them. She wasn't that mad. But even so, she could not forgive herself. She had made a mess of things and she wondered why.

As she gazed at the wall of the small supermarket, reading the advertisements for dog roll and washing powder, she was suddenly reminded of how alone she was. In general she didn't mind being by herself – it was a familiar enough experience – but every now and again – now, for example – she found the thought of her 'aloneness' unbearable. A fleeting image passed through her head: a picture of herself sitting on the couch next to her mother. She imagined her mother's arm around her shoulders, pulling her close, as her soft voice whispered, 'Don't be scared.' But they were words her mother had never spoken, just as the words 'I'm sorry' were not in her mother's vocabulary, Matilda thought.

Her thoughts lingering on her childhood, she was reminded that with the exception of those few weeks spent in the stranger's care, she had always been the one doing the comforting and apologising. It had been her small arms reaching out and not quite meeting around Charlotte's shoulders as she hugged her tight and whispered, 'Don't be scared.'

From the moment her mother had returned 'cured' from the

private hospital, Matilda had done everything in her power to ensure that she would never leave again. She had tried to anticipate every mood, read every nuance in her mother's voice and understand the meaning of every glance. She had done all she could to keep her mother happy, to stop her falling back into the murky hole named 'depression'. She hadn't been old enough to understand what depression was; all she knew was that it had the strength to absorb her mother, to smother her and turn her eyes to glass.

For so many years her mother was defined by depression and then, recalled Matilda, her doctor had finally succeeded in finding the right combination of treatment – a mixture of counselling and drugs that really did seem to offer a 'cure'. Her mother became human again. She smiled. She got dressed in the morning, even had her hair styled once more. Yet despite all this, Charlotte never found it in herself to look her daughter in the eye and apologise. Even after she had moved to Banana and created a new home for herself – one that included a new husband and a son – she didn't once take Matilda in her arms and say sorry for all the years of hell she had put her daughter through.

As a young adult Matilda understood that what had happened was not due to her being a particularly bad daughter so much as to a chemical imbalance in her mother's brain. Yet, she had continued to feel responsible for her mother's mental state and had repeated, over and over and over again, the word 'sorry', apologising to her mother time and time again, as if that might release her from the pain of her childhood. And despite the fact that half the time she only said it in the hope that her mother might reply in kind, Matilda never once heard those words from her mother's mouth. Her mother refused to acknowledge what had happened; she would not take responsibility for all those years of shared misery.

It took only a few minutes to walk from the supermarket to Jacob's house, where Matilda collected her bicycle and set off towards the motel, her new home. She arrived as the streetlights flickered on, their orange glow casting a shadowy light over the deserted forecourt.

She liked her motel unit. It was, she thought, one of the best places she had ever lived. Everything in the room was there for a purpose; there was nothing 'extra' and certainly none of the things she had grown up with: art objects, African masks, cast glass vases, big photographic books. The motel room contained none of the things that had made her feel anxious as a child. Her days in Takapuna had been filled with fear. She had been so frightened of bumping into one of her mother's precious objects that she had anticipated the dull loathing in her mother's eyes every time she walked from the living space to the kitchen. By contrast, the motel lacked character; it held no associations of 'home' for her. Not even the home she had shared with Jacob, the shabby furniture and the clutter filling the hallway. In fact, she noted, looking around, her unit seemed even less homely than the hospital room she had occupied in Gladstone.

Matilda was sitting at the motel table when she heard a car pull up outside. She listened intently, her hand poised above the diary she had started writing, trying to remember incidents from the past week with which to fill the blank pages. Although it was a motel, she felt irritated by the intrusion on her space. She had come to regard the place as her own and up until now had enjoyed being the only occupant in the block. During her stay she had created an evening routine for herself, one that had drawn to a close each night with the sound of gravel crunching beneath the motel proprietor's shoes as he set out to retrieve the spinning 'Vacancy' sign from under a lamppost at the end of the street.

She continued to listen as a single car door opened and closed, a sound followed by the heavy tread of its occupant – a man, she guessed. Although she had been anticipating it, she jumped as the office bell sounded – a loud, shrill noise that could be heard throughout the whole complex. Silence followed, then she heard the muffled voices of two men, the closing of one door, the turning of the key in another – the room next to hers, followed by the same heavy tread as the new occupant inspected his three rooms before returning to the kitchen area and opening the fridge. So close was the sound that Matilda could hear the man place his small jug of milk on the shelf of the otherwise empty fridge before closing the fridge door and placing his keys on the bench. She heard the motel owner's voice, asking the new occupant if he wanted a cooked or continental breakfast, then the room fell quiet, the only noise the sound of footsteps outside, the fading sound of the motelier returning to the office and the guest going to his car.

Still sitting at her table, unable to continue with her reading, Matilda murmured the name Edwin and smiled. Though she had no proof, she *knew* it was him. She glanced around her room and her smile broadened into a grin. At that moment she felt nothing so much as gratitude – the relief of someone offered a second chance.

For some reason it did not dawn on Matilda that Edwin might be surprised to see her standing on his doorstep. Indeed, during the past thirty minutes she had rehearsed her 'casual', unplanned visit to his unit so thoroughly that she had managed to convince herself he would not only be expecting her but would already have the jug on to boil and ripped open a packet of biscuits. She had completely failed to acknowledge that he would have no idea what she was doing there. It therefore took her by surprise to see a look of incomprehension and, she thought, alarm cross his face. Seconds passed before he so much as uttered her name. 'Matilda?' followed by another puzzled silence. Eventually, still clearly confused, he asked, 'Did you leave something in the car? I haven't come across anything.'

So unscripted was his response that Matilda immediately lost her confidence and began to turn away. Yet, even as she retreated, some small part of her continued to believe that Edwin would understand why she had visited. And that part also imagined he would supply the words she needed; that he would invite her inside with the statement 'I've been thinking about your proposal – and the answer is Yes.' Not that she had made a proposal. She had hoped Edwin might be able to explain what it was she was doing.

Confronted with his continuing silence, however, she became more and more nervous and, like some elderly British relative warned not to mention the war in front of a German guest, she found herself raising the one topic she had wanted to avoid. In a voice that seemed to her obscenely loud she demanded, 'What's the scoop with your mother?'

What she expected to happen next she had no idea. Not one of the problems facing her now had arisen during her rehearsal in preparation for this visit. Although in normal circumstances she would have chosen this point to flee, she discovered that her desire to be with Edwin was powerful enough to stop her escape. His silence, however, was disconcerting, and as the seconds ticked by she became increasingly self-conscious and tongue-tied.

It suddenly struck Matilda how cold the night was. Looking up, she saw that the sky was clear and the stars appeared not so much as individual points of brightness but as a glowing milky spill across the night. The Milky Way, she thought, before saying aloud, 'I don't blame you for not talking about your mother. I don't like mine either. In fact, I hate her.' As the words escaped into the night she heard an inner voice remonstrate, 'No, no, no. You've gone too far.' Blushing deeply, her cheeks hot, warmed as if by fire, she mumbled, 'Sorry. I don't want to know, anyway.' She fell silent and experienced a moment's calm. If only words could make her feel the same way, she thought. If words made sense the way silence did, things would be so much easier. Instead, she had a brain full of complicated ideas and a mouth that was barely more sophisticated than that of a talking doll.

Intent on changing course, she observed, 'Cold, isn't it? I should have put my jacket on.' Then, fearing that she might have appeared rude once more, she added, 'When you look up at the sky you get a feeling like vertigo, don't you? I was thinking it would be nice, wouldn't it, if every now and again you could just fall upwards. You know: if you could literally escape into the night. I'd like to do that. I could even film it.'

Glancing across to Edwin, Matilda felt more and more dejected. She had no idea what he was thinking. In the gloom his face appeared completely expressionless but she thought she heard him murmur, 'I watched you film the leaves at the vineyard.' She waited, hoping he would continue and say something to confirm what she thought she had heard, but instead he relapsed into silence, his eyes focused somewhere on the night sky. Suddenly Matilda no longer cared about what might happen next. She could say any old rubbish now, and he could stand staring at the Milky Way for the rest of the night if he wanted. She started to speak again when Edwin stopped her. 'I didn't hate my mother. I could never hate my mother.'

Matilda didn't know how to respond. Probing for more details seemed out of the question, and yet ignoring his remark seemed equally inappropriate. Perhaps, she thought, she should leave. But this in itself raised certain problems because if Edwin remained in his doorway he would find out she was living in the unit next door. She'd have to pretend to leave the complex and then wander around for a while before sneaking back, and she couldn't be bothered. It was just too ridiculous. Sighing, she dug the toe of her shoe into the gravel, turning the frost-covered stones with her foot until a black circle appeared in the dirt. 'Frost,' she observed. 'I'm cold.'

'Come in for a minute and warm up.' Stepping aside, Edwin allowed her to go first, following her into the unit and closing the door behind them. The room was not much warmer than the forecourt. Glancing around, Matilda quickly surmised that Edwin's room was identical to her own, right down to the wood veneer wall-mounted fan heater that gushed warm air into the room. Standing with her back to the heater, Matilda could feel her jeans begin to heat slightly but her body remained as cold as before. She watched as Edwin moved around the room, walking into the kitchen area to fill the kettle, running water from the tap into its spout rather than taking its lid off. That was how Jacob filled it, too, she thought absently as she watched

Edwin remove two tea bags from a plastic canister and place them into a pair of mugs. Edwin stood quietly, the palms of his hands pressed against the steel benchtop as he waited for the jug to boil.

'So, when are you going to make your documentary?' Edwin asked.

Taken aback by the abrupt nature of the question, Matilda started, unable to think of a quick response. Her eyes on Edwin, she searched his face for some indication of what he was thinking, of where the conversation might lead, but she could not fathom his intention. His silence now as he filled each cup with boiling water made her wary. It was all she could do to mutter 'Thanks' as he passed the mug to her.

Her eyes remained on the tag hanging over the side of the cup. She took the damp paper in her fingers and jiggled it once or twice and then let it drop, obscuring the face of the kitten printed on the mug's surface. She was aware that Edwin had sat down at the table, but he appeared quite content to drink his tea without attempting to make further conversation. Catching his eye, she was surprised to see him smile in her direction. 'I'm not sure,' he began, 'how you would go about making a documentary about both old people and stars.'

'I wouldn't,' she responded, surprised by the sudden coolness in her tone. 'I'd stick to people.'

'Oh, I liked the idea of a film about stars.'

Matilda frowned. Although there was nothing at all in his voice to suggest it, she thought Edwin was mocking her. She decided to finish her tea and go. There was no point in staying and, in any case, she couldn't remember why she had thought visiting was such a good idea. Yet, encased in her irritation was a sense of injustice. Edwin had no right to make fun of her. She would defend herself.

'I *need* to make a documentary,' she started, wondering at the simplicity and truth of the remark. It was difficult to explain, this need of hers: her desire to concentrate on something that had the potential to take her away from herself, to forget about herself – for just a short while. For once, she wanted to be an observer rather than a participant, that was all.

Aware that Edwin was waiting, and that she hadn't yet explained herself – and yet feeling reluctant to reveal too much – she said only, 'I think making a documentary might make me feel happy, that's all. That's enough.'

She saw Edwin nod and felt calmer. Perhaps she had been wrong in thinking he was making fun of her. There was a slight chance he might actually be interested.

Anticipating that Edwin might try to draw her out in some way, she was somewhat surprised to see him suddenly stand up and walk back to the kitchen bench. He stood still, appearing to be lost in thought or working on some problem, she thought. She watched as his face contorted into a frown, suggesting he was in the final stages of reaching a decision, and then he appeared to slump and relax slightly, as if the tension that had been mounting had suddenly found a release. At that point she saw him reach into his pocket and withdraw the piece of yellow paper Richard had passed him that afternoon. Smoothing it gently on the bench, he spoke calmly, pointing to the names of the two women as he did so.

At first she didn't understand what he was saying. Too many pieces seemed to be missing from his story. Then after a while it became clearer. He believed that one of the two women was his mother. Might be his mother. He hadn't seen her for many years. He had lost touch with her. As he said 'lost touch' he smiled the same haunted smile that she had seen earlier in the day. In fact at that moment it appeared as if he had lost touch with touch itself. As if he had not felt the warmth of another human for many years.

It was several seconds more before she registered what he was saying: 'I'm trying to find my mother.' He looked embarrassed, as if looking for one's mother was a not entirely decent occupation for a man of his age. 'I suppose,' he added simply, 'I need to find her.' He smiled, aware he was echoing Matilda's words. 'I think finding her might make me happy, that's all.'

For several seconds neither of them spoke or moved. Matilda remained with her back to the heater and Edwin remained standing by the bench. The tension that had disappeared earlier began to creep back into the room, working its way around their bodies, isolating them. Matilda had the feeling that Edwin had not finished, and although she was conscious that something important might be about to happen, she wasn't sure she wanted to be involved. There was something about Edwin – the way he was standing, his expression, the atmosphere of loss that surrounded him – that made her feel uneasy. It was too familiar. She had spent many years guarding against such emotions and being so close to Edwin now suddenly struck her as potentially harmful. She wouldn't stay. That much was clear.

'Maybe,' said Edwin, his voice cutting through the silence, 'you could come with me and make a documentary.' The stillness in the room grew thicker, the only sound the weak whirl of the fan heater. 'My mother would certainly be old – in her eighties – if she's still alive, that is.' A slight noise like a strangled laugh caught in Edwin's throat and he spluttered, coughing a thin spray of tea across the bench.

Matilda stared hard at him, searching his expression for a sign of his intent. He might, she thought, be toying with her. The whole thing could be a joke. But even as she allowed that thought to slip by, she knew he was not joking. She watched as Edwin began to talk once more, this time in a lighter tone, as if trying to camouflage the gravity of his earlier remarks. He couldn't guarantee, he smiled, that he was filmworthy. But if she wanted, she was welcome to tag along.

'You can name your project "Watching an old man make a fool of himself".' He smiled.

Overcome by nerves, Matilda laughed. 'You're not old.' Even as she spoke, she was aware that her words were no match for the thoughts that were hovering around her. The discrepancy between the turmoil inside her and the calm presenting itself to the outside world had been this pronounced only once before in her life: during that brief visit to the doctor's surgery, when he had reached across the table and shown her her test results. Now, like then, she had smiled, but crumpled inside.

Seconds passed as they watched each other in silence, then Edwin said, 'Have you got your camera here?'

Matilda felt embarrassed, as if she had been caught acting unprofessionally. 'No,' she replied, 'it's next door.' Aware that he didn't understand, she explained that she lived next door; that ever since breaking up with Jacob she had been renting the unit next to his; that, in effect, this motel was her home.

Simply uttering that truth made her feel reckless. She could hear a voice inside urging her to agree to Edwin's proposal, to stop making excuses and just get on with it. She didn't need to be so cautious, said the voice. Nothing would happen. It would be fun. As the voice continued to taunt her, growing increasingly impatient with her failure to accept Edwin's offer, Matilda stirred and answered, 'I'll gather my things together and meet you in the morning.'

In her confusion she almost failed to notice that Edwin was still looking at her and smiling. They stood opposite each other: two innocents, she later thought, about to embark upon the unknown.

PART THREE

edwin +
matilda

Edwin, I don't want to think about it, much less talk about it, but I guess if we're going to spend some time together you'll have to know what's going on – why I have so many pills and what I'm taking them for. I have the feeling you're the type of man who would never ask – not because you're too polite (though that, too) but because you would pick up on the fact that there are some things I don't want to discuss. I'm not ready to tell you how I got sick or how I found out. Whatever you can imagine, it was a hundred times worse. That knowledge is mine alone at the moment, and that's just the way it is. That's how I live with it.

But you will need to know that I am HIV positive. That's what all those pills are for. And then there are the other pills – the ones that make it possible for me to cope with the side-effects. Pills for treating the virus, pills for treating the side-effects of the first lot of pills, painkillers for my headaches, pills for diarrhoea or constipation – and there should be one more bottle of pills: the ones that block the thoughts that go through my head, the thoughts that never ever leave me in peace. Those thoughts are like sludge that has settled in my brain – I can never get rid of it: rotting leaves and fetid water in a drained swimming pool.

I try not to think about it but that's a joke, really. How can it be otherwise? Every few hours I have to take one pill, then another and another. How can I not think about it? That's the way it is.

ONE

Matilda woke with a start, her hands balling into fists, which jerked towards her chin, a gesture both of defence and attack. Even as she knew she would try to fight off her attacker, she understood that she was too late. He would have taken advantage of those first anxious seconds, those moments between sleeping and waking, when she had struggled to make sense of the shadow in her room. For her to stand a chance, her attacker would have had to be as surprised as she was. Otherwise, he'd be on top of her before she'd even had a chance to move, or cry out. He would have got her.

There was no one in the room. There was no attacker. She knew that, of course, but she checked all the same, looking around the deserted bedroom, her eyes scanning the furniture, the curtains, looking for movement. The room was undisturbed; no one was there.

Matilda lay still, her eyes resting on the doorway that led into the kitchen/dining area. She wanted to be able to laugh at herself but she was still too scared. The moment for laughter had not reached her yet. In its place was the sense that she was not out of danger. Something was wrong. Waiting for her pulse to return to normal, she closed her eyes, thinking of the day ahead. She knew what to expect; she had experienced so many of these days before – days she referred to in the simplest of terms as 'scary days'. In those first seconds of gaining consciousness she had been overcome by fear. And that anxiety would stay with her now for the rest of the day, running parallel to the events of the next twenty-four hours. It didn't matter that she had things to look forward to, that today she would leave the motel and begin her journey with Edwin – she would still feel scared.

But she could look after herself. All she had to do was get through the day and tomorrow things might be completely different. Tomorrow might be easy by comparison. Even as that thought passed through her mind she felt herself begin to relax.

Through the wall of her unit she heard a slight scuffle followed by the sound of footsteps. It was Edwin. In the night she'd woken once or twice and been aware of a muffled sound coming through the wall near her head. It was, she'd realised, the sound of him sleeping. Less a snoring sound than a murmuring. She'd felt comforted by his presence, the fact that he was so close, their beds pressed head to head, separated only by a concrete block wall. And now he was awake, walking around his room, preparing for the day ahead. She made no move, imagining that she would give him a head start; that no matter how quickly he was able to get ready for their departure, she would be able to catch him up, she would be quicker. She had always been organised.

At boarding school, back in Gladstone, she had often been taken aback by how slow the girls in her dormitory had been when it came to preparing for the day. They moved slowly, reluctantly, as if each felt a need to perform or at least communicate just how much more difficult it was for them to face the day than it was for the next girl. 'Look at me,' each teenager seemed to say. 'I'm so tired. I don't know if I can do this any more.' Girls who in different circumstances would have been no-nonsense, practical farm girls became, in boarding school, self-absorbed and needy. They formed groups: communities that she was never invited to join. But she had liked being alone. It was restful to be apart from the others, to feel responsible to no one, to feel free from the obligation of taking care of another person. For the first time in her life she had felt a sense of calm. A world free from drama. But it hadn't lasted, had it? she murmured to herself as she dressed. Really, it was just the start.

She had to be careful now. If she wasn't careful she would spend the day torturing herself. It was so easy to slip back into that frightening place. She had to protect herself and get out. Yet, as she stood before the bathroom mirror, willing herself to visualise the day ahead – safe images: the white centre markings on the road, Edwin's expression as he concentrated on driving, the sound of the gravel crunching beneath Knowles' shoes as he crossed the parking area to put out the motel vacancy sign – she found other pictures edging into her thoughts. The refrigerated truck. The carcasses of frozen meat that hung from hooks and brushed against her body as she was pushed inside. The headlights of a passing car blanked out by the clunk of the door being kicked shut.

'Stop,' she murmured. 'Stop it now.' She wasn't talking to the man in her memory but to herself. She was telling herself to calm down, and now she would tell herself to turn on the shower and step in and stand beneath the droplets of water that were never quite hot enough to warm her, and she would tell herself to wash her hair and she would wash her hair. Then she would think about something else. The soap. The thin white tablet of motel soap. Public toilet soap. She would think about what she could see, right now, in this bathroom, and she would decide what to wear and whether or not she could be bothered shaving her legs. She would keep her thoughts focused on this room, the unit, the motel, the street, the town, her journey, her documentary. And Edwin. She would think about Edwin and imagine him, just like her, getting ready for the day. That's what she would do. She would not allow her thoughts to stray.

My thoughts lingered on the sensation of brushing a stray eyelash from Matilda's cheek. To tell the truth, I had not touched anyone for a long time. Well, that's not exactly true: my profession entailed a certain amount of contact – it was all part of getting the best possible pose for a subject. But eyelashes. The whispered sound of the word itself suggests fragility, even tenderness. There was a man at the sanatorium when I was a child who used to get teased about his 'doe eyes'. I had never seen a doe but my mother had seen them in the forests in Scotland and she explained that their eyes were a lot like cows' eyes – but sadder. I didn't understand that at the time, though it made sense once I saw *Bambi* at the cinema in Dunedin years later.

The man in the sanatorium had much to be sad about. He had been there for eighteen months and in all that time he had seen his infant daughter only once. The child's mother, a quiet woman, had been terrified of exposing her daughter to the 'white plague', as she called TB. I remember the woman well because whenever she visited she would sit towards the foot of the man's bed – or, if he was sitting up, slightly behind him, as if she was a hairdresser talking to her client but without the aid of a mirror.

My father was also a cautious man. Certain areas of the sanatorium were off limits, and as it never occurred to me to disobey him, there was never any problem. He did allow me, however, to visit the residents who were well on the road to recovery. They posed no risk – they no longer coughed, they weren't infectious. The patients who had been at the sanatorium a long time would sit outdoors or stroll about the grounds in the afternoon. Some were fit enough to undertake light chores, working in the gardens or on the farm, and some even trained as nurses. The patients who could stand the isolation and who had found satisfying work in the sanatorium rarely left.

My father worked long hours, so I spent a great deal of my free time alone, playing in the gardens. My best friend at the time was a man of twenty-eight. His name was Samuel and he'd been sent home from the war, admitted to the sanatorium and stayed on – working on the farm, tending to the vegetable garden and the bees. He had been a 'strongman', a power-lifter, I suppose. He used to show me photographs and newspaper clippings of himself, his muscled body popping out of the woollen vest and briefs he wore as he raised a huge block a few inches from the ground. He'd lost all his strength with the onslaught of TB but even so, he struck me as stronger and healthier than anyone else I knew.

He loved to talk and he would entertain me with stories – which I believed were true – about his stint in the jungle. 'There I was,' he'd frequently begin, 'Nips on one side, man-eating beasts on the other.' He'd smile as he spoke – probably from the pleasure of reeling me in; I was an easy catch. 'I remember the night one of our planes came down. I could see the glow from the flames reflected in the night sky, but it was a long way away and I knew the jungle was all but impassable: if the tigers didn't get me, the snakes would.' I would follow him as he talked, tripping on the back of his boots whenever he paused or changed pace. I was so eager to hear his yarns – I craved his stories: tales of real men rather than the gaunt-faced, coughing and spitting wrecks I shared my home with. 'I fought my way through the night. From time to time, I would catch sight of a pair of gleaming yellow eyes and my blood would run cold. Was it a tiger? Or a slitty? It was impossible to distinguish between them . . .' I remember that word: slitty. I'd heard 'Nips' and 'Japs' but never before had I heard 'slitty'. It was the first – and only – time in my life I'd felt mesmerised by a word. 'Slitty.' It described the Japanese so perfectly. Remember, I was only a child.

Everything Samuel said was that much better than anything anyone else said. I believed everything. The more outrageous the story the more certain I was of its veracity. He was a storyteller. And, more than my father, he was my hero. I adored my father but I idolised Samuel.

One day, during morning tea, a half-eaten hokey-pokey biscuit in his hand, Samuel lifted down his gun, walked out the door and across to the beehives, where he shot himself. Dead.

TWO

'This film of yours,' said Edwin, 'is it a silent movie?'

Matilda jumped at the sound of his voice. It took her a moment to collect herself and even then she felt puzzled. 'What?'

'Well, it's just that we've been driving for fifteen minutes and in all that time you haven't said a word. Not that I'm saying a documentary about roadside posts and flattened rabbits couldn't be interesting but – call it vanity, or delusion – I had the impression that you might want to ask me some questions.'

Edwin smiled as he spoke, hoping that the expression on his face would reassure Matilda. It was true, she had barely spoken a word since leaving Ranfurly, and before that, as she was leaving her motel unit, he had the strong impression she might change her mind and not accompany him after all. He would have felt disappointed. He liked the idea of her company – it took the pressure off him and made him less nervous. Now the search for his mother could be described as a project. He would be the conduit through which Matilda realised her dream to make a documentary and, as such, he would stand back and observe. He breathed a sigh of relief and smiled again. Concluding he was embarking on an adventure of sorts, he decided that once it was finished, the loose ends tied up and tidied away, he would get on with his new life: his life of leisure.

'Do you have any questions?' he asked again, after waiting several seconds for Matilda to respond.

'That's okay with you?' she asked.

It was all Edwin could do not to snort. He had come to expect a certain amount of shyness from her, he thought fondly, but this was too much. The girl needed help.

'Sure it's okay,' he replied. 'I'd be disappointed if you didn't ask questions.'

She still looked unsure, so he prompted her again. 'Come on, ask away.'

A few more seconds passed and then he noticed out of the corner of his eye that the video camera had been turned to face him, a red light indicating she was recording.

'Edwin,' he heard her ask, her voice a strange mix of the hesitant and the formal, 'you've recently discovered that your mother may still be alive, and not dead, as you were led to believe. Why do you think she left you and why do you think your father lied to you all these years?'

Edwin's smile froze on his face. What he had expected Matilda to ask, he didn't know, but the abruptness of this question caught him off guard – he didn't know what to say. He could feel his mouth open and shut once or twice as if he was gulping for words – but even so, no response seemed possible.

Sensing she might have gone too far, Matilda began fidgeting, shuffling in her seat and looking awkwardly from Edwin to the camera and back. Unsettled by his silence, she blurted, 'How do you know she intended to stay away forever? Maybe she wanted to come back for you – you know. Maybe something stopped her?

I mean, my mother always came back for me, whenever she left – I mean eventually she came back.'

Edwin said nothing. Looking past her recorder, which was still focused on his face, Matilda saw his hands tighten their grip on the steering wheel, and then she watched as he let his left hand drop to the gear lever and, for no reason, change from fifth to third. Immediately the engine screeched. Edwin's hand returned automatically to the lever as he changed back to fifth. 'Sorry,' he said, before falling back into silence.

The sound made by the wheels changed. The steady, low hum of smooth asphalt gave way to tinkling as fine gravel sprayed from the tyres. Glancing through the window, Matilda saw frost, thick on the verge yet thinly spread over the road itself. Tyre tracks from previous cars marked a route, cutting black lines through the sprayed-on whiteness, and then the car cleared the shade from the shelterbelt and the ice disappeared, the road humming once more.

Clearing her throat, Matilda asked, 'What are you going to say when you see her?'

Those were her questions. That was all she wanted to know.

Edwin's voice was so quiet, she was unsure she had heard correctly.

'Stop,' he mumbled. 'Stop, please.'

Ashamed, Matilda lowered her camera and rested it on her knee. Yet, even as she did so, a spark of anger flashed in her head. You wanted me to ask questions, she wanted to protest. Did you think I was just going to ask you about the weather? Recognising the childishness of her reaction, she checked herself and tried desperately to think of something to say, something that might save the situation.

'My mother,' she began, 'left me twice. Once because she was depressed and once because she felt like it.' The bitterness in her voice surprised her. Having started to talk about her family, however, she felt she should continue. 'My father left too – but then he was never there in the first place so it doesn't really count.'

She fell silent, aware that the pain in her head from earlier that morning was returning, stronger than ever. Entering Oturehua, she asked, 'Would you mind stopping for a moment? I'd like to buy a drink if that's all right.'

She had expected Edwin to wait in the car but he followed her inside the historic store, looking at the objects on display in the shop's museum. Then, sidling over to the counter, he asked for a mutton pie. Turning to her as he pulled out his wallet, he asked, 'Do you want one?' She shook her head but allowed him to pay for her bottle of orange juice before following him out of the building and taking a seat beside him on the bench outside. It was still cold, the seat and wall behind their backs chilling them further.

Fumbling in her pocket, Matilda took out two painkillers, swallowing them down with a gulp of juice. She grimaced and sat quite still, her eyes closed against the weak sun that eased above the fertiliser shed opposite.

'Are you all right?'

She nodded in response to Edwin's question but was afraid of opening her mouth for fear of gagging. The smell of his mutton pie was making her feel sick; it was overpowering – she could all but taste the thick grease in the back of her throat, the globs of meat in her mouth and the fatty pastry crumbling with each bite. The smell reminded her of her childhood in

—139—

Banana: mutton chops frying in the pan each morning as her stepfather, Sandy, prepared his breakfast. Even after her 'cure' her mother never got out of bed before nine, long after everyone had left the house for the day. When she did finally appear she was always immaculately dressed; her ability to wear a pressed white shirt and keep it spotless for an entire day was legendary among the inhabitants of the small community. The red dust that coated every surface, every item of clothing as a matter of course seemed unable to take hold on her mother's outfits. Even her nails remained clean. Where Matilda's own nails were dust-stained, rimmed with blood-coloured grit, her mother's nails were 'cosmetic-counter clean', as Matilda referred to them. Nothing touched her mother. Nothing.

Thinking about her mother, Matilda began to slip back into the state of anxiety she had experienced earlier that morning. She had thought she had got a hold of things but the image of her mother's white shirt was enough to bring it all back. The white shirt had been one of the first things she'd seen when she'd woken in the hospital. Standing by her bed dressed in a white coat had been a doctor, but behind him, some distance away, stood her mother, her shirt gleaming and making the doctor's coat appear grey by contrast.

She recalled her mother's first words. Coming closer, Charlotte had bent over her daughter and whispered, 'My God, what a mess.' Matilda assumed her mother was talking about her appearance – the dirt on her skin, her rumpled hair – but later, years later, she had softened her view, allowing that her mother might have been trying to comfort her – that she was talking about the 'situation', rather than the lack of cleanliness. Matilda wasn't sure, though. She had never been able to understand her mother. Never. Nothing her mother did made sense.

'Are you all right? Are you sure?'

Again Matilda nodded. If Edwin could just be quiet for a moment, if he could just leave her in peace, she could haul her way back to the present. Submerged as she was now, on the seabed of her past, she needed to get herself back onto the boat, where she could be safe.

'I'm sorry for what happened back there. Your questions came as a bit of a shock. I wasn't expecting . . . I don't know what I was expecting . . .' Edwin's voice trailed off. Changing the topic, he asked, 'Do you feel any better? Is there anything I can do?'

Her eyes closed, Matilda suddenly felt a hand resting on her arm, just below her shoulder. Startled, she sat upright, staring into Edwin's eyes.

'I'm not sure about this,' said Edwin, waving his hand around as if the street in front of him was the problem. 'I can't believe I have allowed myself to think about my mother for so long and yet, despite everything, I still don't have a clue about what I'm going to say when I see her – or her friend Violet, for that matter. Surely I could have worked something out by now, don't you think?' He paused and glanced at Matilda, even though he knew she wouldn't answer. 'After all, it's quite feasible that Violet has never heard of me; she might not know I exist. What's more, she might not believe me . . . What do you say in situations like this? It's beyond me.'

He smiled, adding apologetically, 'You're not getting this on film . . .'

'I thought I'd better wait for the hair and make-up team to

turn up.' Matilda's gaze drifted slowly over Edwin's face and then she turned away, equally embarrassed. 'Sometimes when you talk, you sound like someone my age. You don't sound . . .'

'Wrinkly? Old?' Edwin interrupted.

'No, not old,' continued Matilda. 'Grown up. Sometimes – like the other day or now, for instance – you talk like I think. It's strange.'

'So I talk like a twenty-two-year-old woman?'

Matilda smiled again. 'Or maybe I think like a sixty-two-year-old man – who knows?'

Edwin shook his head slowly before licking the last trickle of mutton fat from the back of his hand. 'No,' he said, 'believe me, you don't.' He paused, screwing up the paper bag and squeezing it tight in his hand. 'I'd have to feel sorry for you if you did.'

My mother sent me to counselling – anything that would save her the trouble of having to talk to me herself. Counselling was legitimate – just as boarding school had been before that.

Boarding school had been her idea. I don't know why I'm telling you this. Perhaps it's because I trust you to keep a secret, or maybe it's because you are asleep, lying in your bed snoring quietly, dead to the world. That's a bit of a film cliché, isn't it? Waiting until someone is asleep before telling them the 'big' story? But now that I'm a documentary film-maker I guess it's okay – even appropriate.

One night, after a long weekend, I was returning to boarding school in Gladstone in a car driven by a couple of guys from Banana. I knew two of them; the third was a stranger. His name was Jon – such a plain name – and he was drunk. I was in the back, squashed between Jon and Nathan. Nathan was also drunk but not as drunk as Jon. Colin was driving. He's the only one I knew, really. We'd been at school together off and on, mucked around – you know how it is. Anyway, I remember the beer cans rolling back and forth on the floor and I remember Colin was singing. He had a great voice – he's a singer now. Does weddings, parties, that kind of stuff.

It was Jon's idea to stop at the pub. None of the rest of us were keen as it was getting late and I had to be back at the school before ten unless I wanted a detention. Sometimes I did want a detention – a detention meant I could get some time to myself, away from the other girls. But anyway we stopped at the pub and Jon jumped out and the other two followed him. I couldn't be bothered – I've never been a drinker – so I just stretched out on the back seat, my back to the door, and looked about. There was a refrigerated truck and six or seven cars in the carpark. The heads of the same number of people were visible through the window to the public lounge: I could see Jon and Colin up at the bar. I couldn't see Nathan. I thought he must be in the toilet.

I remember it was really hot. The back of my top was wet and kind of sticking to the panel in the door. I must have been sitting like that for five or so minutes before the door was suddenly yanked open and I fell half out of my seat. My hair – it was long then, waist length – was in the dirt and I was looking upside down at a guy I had never seen before. He said, 'Gidday, darlin',' before grabbing me by my ponytail and dragging me out of the car.

I guess if my hair had been short, he would have simply found something else to grab hold of, but for some reason I blame my long hair for making it easy for him. My shoes, I recall, scuffed along the ground and one fell off – I'd untied the laces.

Maybe I'd been preparing myself for an event like this all my life, the way all girls do, so as soon as he began dragging me I started to fight. Nothing too bad had happened up to that point and there was a chance I could struggle free and then kill the bastard. Playing in the back of my mind was something I had seen on television – a documentary about prisoners of war and how one of them had said the best time to escape was during transportation from one camp to another. There were fewer guards, fewer obstacles, no fences, so it was the best chance one had of getting away. He hadn't said anything about escaping and then killing your attacker, but that's what I was going to do. At that point I wasn't scared. The fear hit me a moment later.

I glanced towards the pub and I could still see Jon and Colin through the window. They were laughing. But that wasn't what scared me. What scared me was seeing Nathan standing at the window, a glass of beer in his hand, looking out over the carpark. Although I could see him as clear as anything, I knew he couldn't see me. When I realised he couldn't see me I went berserk. I know there's no such word, but I 'berserked'.

My attacker got me to the refrigerated truck, swung open the back door and a wave of freezing air swept over me. Hanging from hooks either side, running the length of the truck, were carcasses. For one crazy moment I thought they were human carcasses: it's a strange fact – pigs can look human sometimes.

I wish I could remember what happened next. I mean, I know what must have taken place, but I don't know what happened. Before I knew anything at all I felt the pain. It was indescribable, but the best way of trying to describe it would be that it felt like someone had put one metal rod into my vagina, another into my arse and then levered me apart. That isn't what happened but that's what it felt like, and it's close enough to the truth.

I heard voices, but even when I woke I didn't realise the voices belonged to actual people. Some nurses were talking about me but it seemed to me they were talking about someone I knew, or had known, until recently. I asked, 'What happened?' and was told, 'You were attacked.' I asked again, 'What happened?' and again they said, 'You were attacked.'

I asked over and over and over again. I couldn't remember

from one minute to the next. I'd been knocked out and because of that I couldn't remember things; I had no short-term memory. Because I couldn't retain things in my head, I kept on asking, 'What happened? What happened? What happened?' Every few minutes, 'What happened?' And every few minutes someone would tell me I had been attacked. It wasn't until the doctor arrived some time later that I heard the word 'raped'.

Over the next six hours I discovered time and time again that I had been raped. No matter how many times my question was answered, I responded as if hearing the news for the first time. It was only when I sensed that people were becoming irritated with me that I shut up.

Colin and Nathan saved my life. They came out, saw that I was missing and heard a noise coming from the truck. Between them, they managed to all but kill the attacker.

For most of that first night I shared a space in intensive care with him – my rapist – we were separated by a curtain. They moved me before they moved him. Apparently he might have died if they'd tried transferring him to the hospital in Gladstone.

I remember two more things: my mother's figure standing in the doorway. She wasn't looking at me but was brushing at some imaginary smudge on her white shirt. She didn't look at me or make eye contact. The other thing I recall is that my father sent me a get well card from China. And a video camera. I'm sorry, Edwin, but I lied about that too. The camera wasn't an engagement present at all.

THREE

'So,' said Edwin, turning off the car engine, 'we're here.' He sat still, his fingers tapping on the steering wheel, then reached for the key and restarted the engine. 'Perhaps we should come back later. She might be having an afternoon rest.'

Matilda glanced past him to the house, which was still some distance away. For some reason Edwin had pulled up two houses away. The distance between them and Violet's house made her feel as if they were staking the joint out – as if they were cops monitoring a house for suspicious comings and goings. It took her a moment to realise that they were the ones behaving suspiciously.

'I'll just drive around the block, check that I'm in the right place.' Lurching into first, Edwin pulled away from the kerb, dawdling past the brick and tile home that was, according to Richard's piece of paper, Violet's.

The 'block' grew larger, taking in the town and then a detour up the hill to the large white clock that was fastened to the cliff face above the township of Alexandra.

Shutting the engine, Edwin asked, 'Have you been here before? I like the view. I find it very peaceful.' It was clear to

Matilda that he was feeling anything but peaceful. Feeling it was her duty to remind him what they had talked about during their approach to Alexandra, she said, 'Remember, you just have to keep it simple: "Good afternoon. My name is Edwin Stubbs. My father was Dr Stubbs, the medical superintendent at the old TB sanatorium above Waipiata. I was there recently and met the current owner blah, blah, blah . . . and I was wondering if I could come in and talk to you."'

Edwin sighed. 'Does that sound convincing to you?'

Matilda nodded. 'Well, you don't look like a salesman or a murderer, if that's what you mean.'

Edwin laughed but his smile quickly evaporated, leaving him silent and gazing pensively through the window.

Matilda was surprised to find herself irritated by Edwin's procrastination. Now that he was her subject, he ought to get on with his search and stop mucking about. On top of which, she was aware that she was running out of videotape and the battery on her recorder would soon need recharging: he was messing her about.

Unable to conceal her irritation, she suddenly said, 'Look, Edwin, just pretend you're an actor . . . pretend it's not you asking the questions and just get on with it. Once you get started it will be easy, I promise.'

Edwin grimaced. 'I bet you said the same thing to your hedge-hog and look what happened to that.'

Matilda laughed. What he said was quite funny.

From the moment Edwin knocked on Violet's door to the moment he discovered Violet was dead took less than one minute. The exchange was over so quickly his heart had no time to quieten in his chest and was still beating rapidly, its echoing drum pounding in his head.

Matilda, who observed the whole incident through her video camera, could not stop herself blurting, 'Dead? She can't be!'

Her voice was so much louder than she had expected, it came as no surprise that the man in the doorway frowned, responding, 'What is this? What's your game?'

It took a few seconds for Edwin to retrieve the situation, explaining once more his reason for searching out Violet – and why Matilda was with him, viewing the events through the lens of a camera.

The man stood nodding and scratching absently at his belly as Edwin spoke, his attitude visibly softening. After a moment he said, 'Wait here . . .' before disappearing back into the house.

Edwin leaned nervously against a brick column supporting the porch and waited. It took several seconds for his nervousness to be replaced by disappointment, but when it finally hit, it made him feel weak, causing him to cling to the pillar for support. Why in heaven's name, he berated himself, had he allowed things to drag on so long? Though it shamed him, the answer was the same as it had been for the past eight years. He wanted his mother to be dead. He had waited because he was scared of finding her – it was that simple. He knew that if he found her, he would want to ask her the one question that had tormented him throughout his life; a question even Matilda could not have imagined. But now that he was faced with the very real prospect that his mother might be finally out of reach, he felt over-whelmed by loss. The truth was, he needed to see her in order to understand.

Suddenly aware that Matilda was being remarkably quiet,

Edwin glanced across to where she had been standing, discovering that she had moved away. It took several seconds to locate her: she had withdrawn to the other side of the road and appeared to be filming the bark of a gingko tree. He watched her for a moment, noticing again the look of concentration on her face that was, by now, almost familiar. She was completely absorbed in what she was doing.

She's not normal, he murmured to himself. Then he noticed how drawn she was looking. Dark shadows gathered like puddles beneath her eyes. Her eyes themselves seemed less bright – dull with fatigue or something else? She had looked quite ill earlier in the day. Perhaps she was coming down with something? But he wasn't sure that was the problem. There was something else. She looked – what was the word? – haunted? Even that didn't seem quite right. It was too dramatic a description. Before he could give it further thought, a voice interrupted. 'Why is your daughter filming a tree?'

Edwin turned as the man continued. 'Don't worry, my son went through a similar weird patch when he was younger. Still, spending the last eighteen months in jail seems to have worked it out of his system . . . Here's Violet's daughter's address and phone number. She lives in Clyde.'

'Pardon?'

The man thrust a torn envelope towards him, 'Violet's daughter. She's my landlady. I've just phoned her at work and she says you can go around this evening, after tea.'

Edwin felt his stomach lurch. Taking the envelope from the man's hand, he focused hard on the name and address scrawled across its surface. Frances Gray. The same surname as her mother's.

'Jesus, don't look so surprised, mate. All it took was a bloody phone call.'

'Can you do it, please? It's better when someone else does it – I always end up cutting myself when I do it.' Edwin had been taken aback by Matilda's request. The idea of him trimming her hair struck him as bizarre. But then the whole afternoon, the events leading up to this moment, were similarly bizarre. The day itself was somewhat surreal.

It had started when they'd left Violet's house. Unable to decide what to do, they had driven around Alexandra for a while, eventually turning into Success Road for no other reason than the fact that its name had caught Matilda's attention. The street came to a dead end but, turning back to rejoin Boundary Road, they found themselves following the wide avenue through the industrial part of town, past sheds and high chain-wire fences before reaching the recycling centre at its far end. It had been Matilda's idea to go in. She'd insisted that it was one of the better recycling centres in the area – as if such things were graded – and had persuaded Edwin to join her in what she laughingly promised to be a treasure hunt.

While Edwin had trailed behind, Matilda scavenged through the shelves and bins before letting out a jubilant exclamation – 'Clippers!' – and rushing back to show Edwin her discovery. He hadn't realised the clippers were intended for her hair and that later, once they had finally reached a decision about how to pass the rest of the day and checked in to a motel, she would pull the clippers out and ask him to cut her hair.

'Your hair is nice, Matilda,' he said by way of protest. It wasn't that he didn't want her to have her hair cut – not that there was much to cut – but that he didn't want to be the one to do it. There were plenty of barbers and ladies' hairdressers around; she didn't need him. But she'd been persistent, sitting in front of him with a pale green towel draped over her shoulders simply waiting for him to begin. She was wearing something like a vest – a tanktop, he supposed – and he noticed as he raised the clippers towards her head that her upper arm was rail thin, her shoulder bony – knobbly like those of the seriously ill patients at the sanatorium. As he rearranged the towel to protect her, his fingertips touched her skin and, fleeting though the moment was, he registered its warmth and recoiled.

'Are you sure about this? I might hurt you,' he stuttered.

He stood behind her, hoping once more that she might change her mind. Then, taking her head gently in his hands, he tilted it, bringing it slowly to an upright position. He weighed the clippers one last time in his hand before turning them on.

'I'll blame you if I get electrocuted,' he muttered.

The clippers were old-fashioned, heavy, enamelled metal and poorly balanced. They vibrated in his hand, sending small pulses through his wrist and up his arm. Though they were noisy and appeared to be on their last legs, he noticed that although they were well worn, they had been well cared for. The blade itself was shiny; it looked as if it had been sharpened many times over the years – probably oiled, too, on a regular basis.

Not knowing quite where to start – Matilda's head suddenly seemed much larger than it had only minutes before – Edwin traced a line from the nape of her neck to the crown of her head. The result was uneven. He was uncomfortable touching her head and held the blade too high – it had hovered above her skull rather than being guided by it.

He attempted another line, creating a second path beside the first, like a strip cut into an unkempt lawn. He paused and breathed out slowly. It was only then that he realised he had been holding his breath. Standing back to survey his work, he asked, 'Are you all right?', to which he received a nodded reply. Then, stepping slightly to his left, he began the third cut.

This time as he worked he brushed the loose hair from Matilda's head. It was an automatic gesture, but as his hand brushed against her neck he started, reawakened once more to the touch of her skin. There was a scar. He hadn't noticed it before – but then how could he have? Now, however, it stood out clearly. A long raised line, a chalk mark scrawled across the shorn pavement of her head and disappearing into the thatch of her longer hair. It was quite a scar, probably dating back to some childhood mishap, he decided. She was the kind of girl who would fall out of trees, he thought. She probably spent a great deal of time playing by herself, building forts and climbing, he felt sure of it.

He cut another line through her hair and noticed that the scar kept growing; he had still not reached the end of it. Whatever she had done, it had almost split her head in two – it was as if she had been scalped. Feeling increasingly uneasy, Edwin continued cutting, saying nothing to Matilda about the scar, which now extended from ear to ear.

He was getting used to the clippers now. He felt as if he had established a kind of rhythm and he was pleased to see that the results were becoming far more professional.

As he worked, Edwin found himself being lulled by the steady drone of the shears. The noise was persistent, like that made by a bumblebee trapped in a room on a sleepy, warm afternoon. Briefly, his thoughts drifted back to his childhood: a memory of sitting in the sunroom watching as his mother read from a book. She used to read a lot, he remembered. She would carry books of verse with her: Wordsworth was her favourite – she could recite his poems by heart. Edwin himself could remember few of the lines – there was the daffodil one, a lot about stars and silence and lonely hills . . . a lot about solitude. She had a tendency, he remembered now, to linger over the word 'solitude'. But if asked to name one poem, he could not. Searching his memory he recalled one line – no doubt because it was short and simple: 'Still longed for, never seen.' He had no idea where it came from; it might not even have been Wordsworth. There were other writers she admired – Shakespeare, Keats, Rossetti, and the man who wrote that famous poem, the one about the nightingale – who was that? Was that Wordsworth too? Or maybe Keats?

His mother had always cut his hair. There was a man, a barber among other things, who lived in the sanatorium, but nevertheless it was his mother who cut his hair. She was so gentle whenever she touched him. She held his head between her hands as if it was an egg and she was scared of cracking it. She had a way of running her fingers through his hair, as if assessing its length, before combing out a piece and clipping it with a pair of his father's medical scissors. The scissors, he guessed now, were intended for cutting gauze bandages or something similar. They were shiny steel, the word Inox hammered into one of the long, tapered blades. They were unusual scissors, certainly he had never seen any like them since.

Edwin recalled the way his mother would guide his head, gently tilting it from side to side as she trimmed, and he recalled the sound made by the scissors, that whispered 'snip snip' as tufts of his hair fell onto a sheet of newspaper placed on the floor.

Once, he remembered, his mother bent down and picked up a piece of his hair and held it up to the sunlight, saying, 'My hair was blonde like yours once.' He couldn't be sure, but he had the feeling she used to pocket strands of his hair, that she kept pieces of it sealed in envelopes in a drawer in her dresser. He was sure of that, now. He had come across one such envelope shortly after she died. Or, rather, shortly after he had been told that she had died. There was only one envelope, labelled 'Edwin, 4½ years old'. The rest, if there had been any more, were gone. Yes, he remembered that now. She kept pieces of his hair. Goodness, he hadn't been conscious of retaining that memory. He wondered what else was locked away in his head.

He was almost finished with Matilda's hair. It was so short it barely coloured the pale skin on her scalp. It was lucky it wasn't summer; she would have had to take care in the sun. What was left of her hair was soft, fur like, barely flattening beneath his touch.

His mother used to wash his hair, too. She never scrubbed at his head the way the nurses did to some of the patients, but she would almost tickle it. She used coal tar soap and it created almost no lather, but it always got his hair clean and the smell would stay with him for days afterwards – it even scented his pillowcase.

Her own hair was mid-length and brown. Were there touches of grey? he wondered. He couldn't be certain, but perhaps, even though she was in her twenties, there were already one or two strands of grey around her temples. Nothing like the grey that now covered his own head but fine strands, like silk threads left by a spider. She kept her hair tied in a bun, letting it down only in the evening, when she would pass a comb through it. She didn't own a hairbrush but the comb, he seemed to remember, was made of ivory – although he couldn't be sure.

Her touch was so gentle when she combed his hair. On Sundays, before church, she would sit him down in front of her, smoothing and combing his hair, and then she would take his head between her hands and kiss it lightly. Even though her lips seemed weightless, he could feel them. A slight press, followed sometimes by an almost imperceptible sigh. In retrospect, there was something sad about that kiss – was it a parting gesture? She never ruffled his hair the way his father did – later, after she died and he was left. No one combed his hair after she was gone. He did it himself. But once every three months it was cut by the barber, the same as everyone else's.

'Edwin?' He imagined her voice calling to him, the way the second syllable rose just slightly – not much, just a little – always a question on his mother's tongue.

'Edwin? Can you just stop for a second?' Edwin started, confused at the sound of Matilda's voice. 'Sorry,' she said, 'but blood's going in my eye – I think you've nicked me.'

Startled, Edwin looked down, the clippers still whirring gently in his hand, as he fumbled to bring his thoughts back to the present. Matilda sat before him, her hand raised to her temple, dabbing at a trickle of blood that oozed slowly from her hairline.

'It's all right,' she murmured. 'They say heads bleed. Heads and feet.'

She didn't know about feet, never having cut them on a broken bottle or a sharp-edged piece of iron – they were not part of her experience. But heads were. Her own head had bled and bled. That's what she'd been told by Colin, anyway. When she'd gone home, no one had mentioned the fact that she'd been raped, but Colin had come around for a visit and during the course of the hour mentioned that she'd bled like a stuck pig – there had been so much blood that neither he nor Nathan could initially work out exactly where it was coming from.

He'd told her, too, that his adrenalin had been pumping and that once she'd been taken away he had all but collapsed, his legs had been wobbling so much. Nathan had it even worse. He was covered in blood – completely soaked, and for a long time the ambulance driver had thought he was injured too. The ambulance driver had kept on trying to get Nathan to get into the ambulance but Nathan had pushed him away, telling him to 'Fuck off!' He was so pumped, said Colin, that he kind of lost it. 'He'd fairly killed that guy, you know – that guy? In fact,' Colin continued, 'Nathan had smashed his hand quite badly: broken his thumb and cut the back of his hand from working the guy over so thoroughly.'

Later, Matilda remembered, when events had run their course and she'd found out about the other thing, she'd seen Nathan in the street and he had spoken to her, telling her he'd been 'called in' – they thought he should have 'the test'. Neither of them needed to say what test; they both knew. Nathan had looked embarrassed: he'd shuffled and not met her eye when he'd said 'they' were worried there may have been some transfer of blood – as a result of the fight. He'd looked even more uncomfortable, she remembered, when he told her he'd been cleared. He was okay, he said: the result was negative.

All the time he spoke, he hadn't raised his eyes to meet hers, but now he did. He glanced at her and in that fraction of a second she saw his whole life – it was there, still in front of him. It was relief. But another thing: when he looked at her his lip trembled, she could see it now – his bottom lip gave way and trembled and he mumbled, 'Sorry.' There was no mistaking what he was thinking – it was only human.

'Sorry,' said Edwin, 'I must have drifted off. I was thinking about something else.'

'It's all right, honestly,' replied Matilda. 'I've had worse . . .'

The room fell silent. For a moment the silence seemed to consume them, each lost in thought, but then as the seconds passed the faintest noise caught first Matilda's and then Edwin's attention. They were both listening, puzzled, though neither made any mention of it at first.

Eventually Matilda asked, 'Can you hear that?'

Edwin nodded. 'It sounds like a frog, doesn't it?' They turned to where the noise was coming from and listened once more. 'But there's no water near here; it can't be a frog,' said Edwin. They remained still, listening, and then the noise disappeared and the room fell silent once more.

Matilda laughed quietly. 'It did sound like a frog, didn't it?' She cocked her head to one side but the sound had vanished. A drop of blood dripped from her brow onto the sheet of newspaper draped across her knee.

'Let me get that . . .' But as Edwin reached to dab the blood from Matilda's face she stopped him.

'No, don't.'

Taken aback by the abruptness of her tone, Edwin hesitated, then, thinking he might have misheard, he reached forward once more, only to have his hand snatched away by Matilda.

'I'll do it,' she said.

There was a moment's awkwardness as both appeared caught mid-flight, but the moment passed; it seemed to fade to be replaced once more by the faint sound of chirruping.

They listened, puzzling over the sound, and then a faint smile crossed Matilda's lips. 'You know what it is, don't you?'

Edwin shook his head.

'It's someone's car alarm . . . it must be miles away.'

They listened quietly, both intent on the sound, slowly making sense of it and feeling slightly foolish. Now that they knew what it was, the noise bore no likeness at all to a frog.

'Do you want me to finish your hair?'

Matilda nodded, this time aware of nothing but the drone of the clippers and Edwin's hands moving gently across her scalp as he worked, slowly and carefully, finishing with the words 'There, done', as his palm settled leaf-like on the crown of her head.

As I get older I find I spend more and more time thinking about my childhood. I suppose I am like many other people in that respect – I believe it's fairly common. I wonder, sometimes, if my recollections of my childhood will stay with me, even when – or if – I'm truly old and senile. I imagine I might lose my short-term memory but I'm not so sure I will forget the sanatorium. If anything, it's fresher in my mind now than it ever was. I suppose that has to do with this search for my mother.

Even though I had been told that she was dead, I used to wait for her to come back. Perhaps, without knowing it, I didn't believe what my father had told me. Now I come to think of it, I was aware back then of the absence of proof: there was no grave. We didn't go to the graveyard even though, at the time, people did visit graves – it was common practice. I have to say, as activities go, that one has always struck me as particularly morbid.

The worst day was the 22nd of September, my birthday. It still is, by the way. On that day I would lie in bed and wait, and I would imagine the door opening slowly – just a crack at first, and then, inch by inch, slowly wider until the opening would reveal my mother's face. The door was a tight fit in the frame; it had been put in before the carpet was laid so it was a difficult door to open. It didn't swing but, rather, dragged across the carpet, wearing an arc across the floral design – neatly bisecting a pink rose.

Because it was such an awkward door I only ever closed it on two nights of the year: the night before my birthday and Christmas Eve. I closed it so that my mother could open it. I wanted to draw out the moment of her return. I didn't want her to appear suddenly at my bedside; I didn't want her to simply 'pop up' – I wanted to be lying in bed waiting, and hear the door open and know that she was behind it. I imagined she would peek into my room and murmur something simple, just 'Happy birthday'. I didn't ever consider that she would have to explain her absence – I wasn't at all interested in hearing about that; I just wanted her to be there, to come back for my birthday.

Matilda, I don't know if you've ever had to wait for something – something so important it defies understanding or definition. I don't know if you understand what it is like to wait for something that has the power to completely transform your life. You're young, so probably not. I can recall the way hope would gradually leave me. I could feel it escape with every breath, and it almost seemed that if I stopped breathing I could 'still' the world, and maybe then my mother would return. The waiting suffocated me. Then it would begin: the questions I must have asked over and over and over again, throughout my life: 'Why wasn't I enough? What was wrong with me?'

FOUR

Edwin was surprised at how quickly he managed to both introduce himself and Matilda to Frances and explain the reason for their visit. Indeed, the introductions and explanations – even the setting up of Matilda's camera – passed so quickly that he found himself feeling strangely lost now that he was sitting in Frances's living room. He had the sense that he would like to replay his arrival so he could be absolutely certain that he was actually sitting in the same room as the daughter of his mother's friend. In the space of too short a time he had found himself in the company of someone who knew his mother and, what's more, knew of him. This woman, whom he had never met before, was the only link he had with his mother, and he found the whole situation somewhat unreal.

He had been pleased Frances hadn't tried to hug him. Hugging was something even strangers did, he knew, but he had never felt comfortable hugging a complete stranger. So when Frances had uttered, 'You look just like Jess!' and taken a step towards him, he had stepped back, knocking into Matilda, who was standing just behind him. Until that moment Edwin had only said, 'Good evening. My name's Edwin Stubbs and this is my companion and documentary-maker, Matilda Muir.' Hearing his voice, he had imagined he resembled a Jehovah's Witness: one of those men who shuffle awkwardly on the doorstep while anticipating the moment of being sent away. He had not expected Frances's reply. That had exceeded anything he had imagined and it had floored him.

Frances, by contrast, had appeared surprisingly matter of fact. Edwin was relieved when she took charge, inviting them in and even clearing a space for Matilda and her camera in the corner of the living room. Then she left them while she fetched coffee.

A few minutes later a young man walked into the room and sat down beside Edwin, saying only 'Hi' before reaching for the remote control and turning on the television. For a full five minutes Edwin watched Sky sports, his eyes fixed on two teams of bikini-clad girls knocking a volleyball from one side of a beach court to the other. From time to time the boy next to him would grunt, but other than that neither of them spoke, and it was only by chance that Edwin caught Matilda's eye and discovered that she was quietly laughing – at him, he guessed. Wishing to escape Matilda's probing eye, if only for a minute, Edwin excused himself, asking where the bathroom was, so that he might retreat into a quiet space where he could be alone while he gathered his thoughts.

As soon as he entered the bathroom he felt calmer. It was an old-fashioned room, painted a dull green, with a bath taking up one entire wall. The basin was also a dull green – a large pedestal type, with room only for soap, two toothbrushes and toothpaste in its small recesses. The soap, Edwin noticed, was also green, but newly opened: its edges were still distinct; they had not yet dissolved or been washed away.

As he washed his hands his mind wandered back to the girls he had just seen on the television. Their bodies, he thought, were so lacking in femininity that they almost appeared constructed. By contrast, almost all the women he had ever photographed appeared deconstructed. His women – the ones who captured his attention – had always seemed somewhat raw, stripped back, like Matilda. He pictured an image from his 'wall of strays' – a photograph of a woman who had come to him before she had a mastectomy. She'd wanted a record of her body, she'd explained – a 'before' image to remind her of what she was, inside. Edwin hadn't completely understood what she meant by 'inside' but he had understood her desire to have a picture of herself and had done everything in his power to make her look beautiful. The truth was, she was beautiful, he remembered.

She'd tried to make light of the session and her operation, saying that she would return in a month or two for an 'after' photograph. She had it all planned: she was going to cover her scar with a tattoo – a climbing rose. She had seen something similar on a woman in a magazine article about cancer. That woman had chosen ivy, but she wanted a rose: 'A rose by any other name . . .' she said, before looking away at something behind Edwin. It had been several seconds before she spoke again. Her eyes glistening, as if, thought Edwin, dew had settled on the rose, she said, 'Who knows? Perhaps I'll look even better after surgery . . .' She smiled, but it disguised nothing.

Edwin had taken her photograph and then waited for her to return for her second sitting. He never saw her again. From time to time he would remember her name and think about her, but not often. In time he almost forgot about her, but then one day he came across a print of her and pinned it to his 'wall of strays'.

She'd watch him as he ate his breakfast each morning, looking down on him as he read the newspaper before work. Her eyes still dewy, she watched him the day he came across her name in the obituaries: *Jill Morton, aged 33. Darling wife of Hamish and mother of Luke, 7; Angus, 4; and Beth, 3. A rose by any other name would smell as sweet . . .*

Glancing at his reflection in the bathroom mirror, Edwin realised he was crying. Not much, and only through one eye, his right – a weak trickle that extended as far as his cheek. Seeing himself reflected in Frances's mirror, he wondered what she had meant when she said he looked just like his mother. In what way did he resemble his mother? Then, with a thud, he absorbed what she had said. She knew his mother – she had *known* her.

Returning to the living room, Edwin was relieved to discover that Frances had not yet returned with the coffee. He needed a minute more, before her return, in order to gather his thoughts. Matilda had not moved; it appeared she had been waiting for him, however, because her expression was one of relief. Now that her hair was shorter – almost non-existent – her eyes looked extraordinarily large and, he thought, even darker than before. He smiled at her as he sat down and she raised her hand in a slight gesture of greeting, then, in a voice that seemed somehow distant, said, 'Charlie says you have twin sisters – half-sisters. One of them lives on the coast, near Franz Josef. We can go there next.'

For a brief moment Edwin wondered if Matilda had broken the news for the sole purpose of being able to record the sight of his jaw dropping with surprise. He closed it quickly and tried to think of something to say, something that might convey the impression that he had control of the situation, but, to his shame, he realised his mouth was simply gaping, and no words were coming out. He was aware of Matilda watching him, and then he was aware that the couch he was sitting on had suddenly lost its substance. It was as if he was no longer being supported; he had the impression he was about to fall through the couch and then through the floor and through the very ground itself. So unbalanced did he feel that he grabbed the arm of the couch, only to discover that rather than touching something solid he had grasped nothing more substantial than a bunch of flowers.

His whole world was falling away, he was collapsing, and yet his heart was beating so loudly he wanted to cover his ears, to protect them from the sound. God knew what he must look like – what image he was conveying for the screen. Surely Matilda wouldn't be filming him now? He glanced towards her and then to Charlie, who, remarkably, was still sitting beside him, his eyes fixed on the television and the women knocking the ball from one side of the net to the other.

At that moment, as Edwin's eyes locked on the volleyball that hurtled through space, Frances finally returned, carrying a percolator and a large rectangular plate displaying sliced salami, cheese, salmon and crackers.

'I thought you might need a snack. We often nibble away during the evenings, don't we, Charlie?'

'Well, you do,' grunted the boy.

'Oh, don't be like that – you know you like to pick at things as much as me.'

Their brief exchange baffled Edwin. He felt he could no longer understand what they were saying. It was not as though he had forgotten English – or all the words contained under that broad heading – but as if he had never learnt it in the first place. He could feel himself wanting to leave the room, to flee, but try as he might, his legs would not co-operate and he sank further and further into his seat, unable to do anything except take the cup of coffee that was offered to him and stare at it in amazement, as if it was some rare artefact that had been entrusted to him for safe keeping.

Frances, however, appeared not to notice as she asked the boy, Charlie, for details about one of the players – a statuesque woman whose shoulders were wider than those of most men.

'I like that one,' said Frances to no one in particular. 'It's hard to believe she gave birth to twins only a month or two ago – by Caesarean of course. None of those women give birth the proper way.'

Not understanding what was expected of him, Edwin automatically lowered his eyes to the player's stomach, but if it was true that she had given birth there was no indication of it – two columns of muscle rippled the length of her taut belly.

'Charlie says they use make-up to accentuate their muscles – isn't that right, Charlie?'

'Yeah,' nodded the boy, his eyes never straying from the television.

'They use a kind of body foundation to draw in contours and shadows – absolutely bizarre, isn't it? God knows you'd think there'd be more important things in the world to occupy your mind . . .'

Charlie grunted once more, then stood up and stretched. 'It's a charity match, to raise money for the animals made homeless by that hurricane . . .'

No one spoke. Even Frances, who seemed very much in control of the situation, sat quietly, mulling over Charlie's announcement. Sipping from her cup, she slowly shook her head, then, looking towards Matilda, said, 'I hope you're getting this – history in the making!' She laughed then and shrugged, before turning to Edwin, who still sat bewildered on the couch.

Her gaze rested on him and she sighed. 'It's your eyes – they're just like hers.' Then, as an afterthought, she added, 'But of course you'll see Jess, so you can find out for yourself.'

It was at that exact moment, Matilda noted, that the cup slipped from Edwin's hand.

Some things don't make sense. A lot of things don't make sense.

During the rainy season thousands of frogs would suddenly materialise out of nowhere and wherever you stepped you would be walking on frogs. At night the noise was incredible. You'd get up to go to the toilet and there'd be at least one or two frogs swimming around in the bowl and the thing is, you'd expect it to be easy to catch a frog in a toilet but it's not at all – they'd dive down and disappear up the U-bend and in the end you'd just have to pee and hope you weren't hitting them on the head – or, worse, that they wouldn't try to leap out and get you on the bum. I don't know what happens once you flush the toilet – I guess that's pretty much the end of it if you're a frog.

Last summer Jacob and I went camping at Wakatipu and there was a sign in the longdrop: 'Rats! Due to a recent infestation of rats we request that you do not dispose of food or rubbish in this toilet. Please keep the lid closed at all times!' Aside from the fact that you can't use a toilet when the lid's closed, I could hardly bring myself to sit on the seat – I was so sure a rat was going to crawl out of the toilet and over my leg just as I was having a shit. It made me realise frogs weren't so bad after all.

I wonder why Edwin's mother left him – why his mother left and mine stayed? I mean, which is more damaging – the mother who tells you she loves you and leaves, or the mother who calls you stupid and stays? My mother once yelled at me: 'How could you be so stupid?' She was referring to my being raped, but she'd missed the point completely. What was stupid was not that I had allowed myself to be raped but that I could be raped and yet somehow regard myself as lucky. That was the stupid part: I'd catch myself thinking, At least I wasn't beaten to death or left severely brain-damaged. The strange thing is that I still believe I am lucky, in a way. I like being alive. Not many people would guess this but I believe in myself – I really do. But it's not much consolation, knowing what I had to go through to reach this point.

FIVE

Matilda could see that Edwin wanted to escape. Even before the accident with the cup he had looked tense – very pale – and he had been too polite. Every word he had spoken had been caged in politeness: it was as if he was sharing morning tea with a tradesman or a distant cousin, someone he didn't know but felt obliged to be on friendly terms with, despite having nothing in common, or nothing to say.

There were times, watching him, when she wanted to say, 'Cut!', or whatever term it was that video-makers used; she felt a strong desire to save him, or protect him – or both. What he was going through – the pain of what he was going through – was too evident and yet Frances could not see it. She gave the impression of being oblivious to his discomfort. She continued to talk about Edwin's mother, and then in a matter-of-fact way brought out some photographs and started shuffling through them, searching for pictures of Jess – almost aggressively.

'Stop for a second. Look at Edwin's face! Can't you see the effect your words are having?' Matilda was tempted to yell, but she refrained from speaking, merely filming as pain burrowed deeper and deeper into his eyes. What the hell was going on?

Frances was being more than thoughtless; she was cruel.

'Look, Edwin. Here's a picture of your mother and Violet with my brother and me at Franz Josef. We often spent the summer with Jess, both before her children were born and after. She had children late in life – she must have been about forty. Here she is with her twins, Beth and Alberta . . .'

'Alberta? My father's name was Albert . . .' mumbled Edwin.

'Was it? Jess never mentioned it . . . but I suppose my mother must have known. She knew more about your mother's past than I did. I wasn't told any of that . . . Jess didn't talk about that.'

Frances's voice trailed off, a brief respite from her continual chatter, before resuming. 'I remember this one . . .' she said, indicating the image at Franz Josef. 'Jess hadn't wanted to come out that day . . . she was very downcast, very quiet. What's the date on the back? I can't read it without my glasses.'

She passed the photo to Edwin and he turned it in his hands and read: 22 September 1965. His eyes fixed on the image, he murmured, 'My birthday – my twenty-first.'

Something in the tone of his voice caught Frances's attention. She hesitated before reaching for the print, and when she held it in her hand she looked at Edwin and murmured, 'I'm so sorry – I had no idea.' She traced the image of Jess absently with her polished fingernail before passing it back. 'You keep it – and I can get prints of any of the others. Just . . . Goodness, I've been pretty insensitive, haven't I? God, what a day.'

Only then, Matilda observed, did things settle down, become more civilised. The pace slowed: Frances offered photographs, spoke gently of her memories of the particular events portrayed, and then passed each image to Edwin, who stared transfixed.

'This is a nice one,' said Frances about one photograph – an image depicting a wedding. 'That's Violet in the bride's dress and my father next to her – and there, do you see, that's Jess – look, she's covering her mouth with her hand . . . she used to do that a lot when she smiled. She was very self-conscious about her mouth: it was slightly disfigured – do you remember that?'

Although Edwin nodded, he said, 'I never noticed. I just thought she was beautiful.'

'Oh,' rejoined Frances, 'she was beautiful – everyone thought so.'

Silence followed, and when Frances spoke again her voice was gentle, with no trace of the businesslike tone of before. 'Jess never spoke about you, Edwin. I only found out about you recently. When my mother was dying she mentioned your name and it was the first time I'd heard it. I'm sorry, but it didn't mean anything to me . . . It was just an incident that occurred during a terrible period in my life. I didn't take much notice, to tell you the truth. It wasn't as if you even seemed real . . . you were just mentioned in passing and I didn't – don't – know any more. I honestly don't know anything more about that period in your mother's life.'

It didn't seem to matter what Frances said now. From where Matilda stood, she could see that Edwin was tattered; he was like some moth whose wings continue to lift in the breeze long after it has been trapped in the grille of a car. She had to take him home.

'I don't want her to feel ashamed,' murmured Edwin.

'No?' And for a moment, the harshness returned to Frances's voice.

Despite the fact that the motel was only twenty minutes from Frances's home, the drive had been uncomfortably long. At one point, in a desperate attempt to cheer Edwin up, Matilda began to tell him about how she met Jacob. She didn't know why the story had popped into her head, or why she thought it might help, but she felt she ought to try to distract Edwin – if only for a moment – and, this being one of the few funny stories she knew, she told it. As she spoke, she realised that the incident didn't sound particularly funny. It was as if the events of the evening had tainted her ability to make an amusing tale sound just that: amusing. Her delivery was flat – she was making something dull of an encounter that had, in reality, been pretty bizarre. She felt disappointed. Even though Edwin did manage a smile, she knew she had wasted a good story.

She'd wanted to know what Edwin thought of Frances, but, although it was a legitimate question given the fact that she was making a documentary, she felt hesitant. Doubt began to creep into her mind: perhaps she wasn't cut out for documentary-making? It was all very well wanting to be a film-maker but what if she wasn't up to the challenge? She couldn't understand how documentary-makers thought: how they managed to make such revealing programmes without being drawn into the lives of their subjects. What did everyone do when the film was finished? She couldn't visualise that part: the moment when she would have to say, 'Thanks for being in my documentary, Edwin – it was great . . . I'll send you a copy when it's finished. Bye . . .' She'd never been much good at ending things; she hadn't even left home until she was eighteen – a remarkable fact given the nature of her relationship with her mother. With the benefit of hindsight she sometimes wondered if she had hung on so long in the hope that things would improve between herself and Charlotte. But she'd been kidding herself – her mother was never going to attempt reconciliation; she would never admit guilt. She was too deeply trapped by denial, and all she could ever do was pile hurt upon hurt until it buried them both.

Matilda remembered the last evening she had spent at home, when her mother had taken her to one side and tried to force her into taking medication. She couldn't recall the exact words of the exchange but she remembered that her mother's attempt had been so hamfisted that at first Matilda had thought her mother was suggesting she overdose on antidepressants. That her own mother was advising her to commit suicide in order to escape from her 'ordeal' did not astound Matilda. It was the type of chilling suggestion she had come to expect from a woman who, for years, had tried to rid herself of her daughter. Yet, Matilda remembered, even though the evening had been warm – they'd been sitting out on the veranda watching the sun set – she had felt suddenly cold, almost as frozen as the carcasses she had seen strung up in the refrigerated truck. It was only the baffled look on her mother's face that had finally saved the situation. It was one of the few times she had seen her mother on the back foot, sobbing pitifully as she babbled, 'No, no – not that . . . All I'm trying to say . . .' And here her mother had all but collapsed, such was her display of remorse. 'I'm just saying I wish I'd been told about antidepressants when I needed . . . when I was such a . . .'

Matilda had been unable to contain herself. 'Why, so you could top yourself and leave me? Well, maybe you should have!'

'No, no . . . I'd never do that!'

Listening to her mother, Matilda had felt herself being manipulated. She could all but see the forked tongue concealed in her mother's mouth.

—175—

'I didn't need you . . .' she said. 'In fact it would have been easier if I'd been alone – I wouldn't have had to look after you, then.'

She'd stared at her mother and watched as her tongue appeared to have been momentarily swallowed. God, her mother was convincing. She should have been an actor; the way she managed to keep up her performance in front of such a small audience – an audience of one – was remarkable. She was so good at conveying emotions; if only she could feel them as well.

'Matilda . . .' Matilda had adjusted her posture, standing erect, a look of hopeful expectation pasted to her face as she prepared for her mother's final dramatic revelation. Sooner or later she knew her mother would begin to talk in clichés. That was the one fault in Charlotte's performances. Having picked up her entire emotional vocabulary from afternoon television, she tended towards over-acting – she couldn't help herself. Her mother didn't understand the concept of 'less is more'. She would lay it on thick; highly charged theatre taking centre stage over sincerity. Matilda's lips curled into a faint smile as she waited.

Misinterpreting her daughter's expression, taking it to be one of encouragement, Charlotte lowered her voice. 'Everything was so hopeless – you've no idea how depressed I was. It wasn't even as if I felt numb – in fact feeling numb would have been preferable to what I felt. I was dead. I failed. At life . . . Matilda . . . everything. My life, everything was wrong . . .'

'Including me, no doubt.' The reply sounded childish but it was the type of remark a 'television' girl in her situation would make.

Ignoring her daughter's remark, Charlotte ploughed on.

'I had no support, Matilda. Business took up so much of

your father's time; he didn't have enough space in his schedule for us. My life, my emotional state, had been manageable before you were born. I used to travel with him and he would take care of me . . . but once you were born I was trapped . . .' Sensing her daughter stiffen, she quickly continued. 'I don't mean you trapped me. I never felt that but . . . it's just, I don't know . . . I couldn't cope. I lost all my confidence and I was just so useless . . . at everything . . . you've no idea.'

'Oh, I think I have,' Matilda scoffed.

'Matilda . . . you've never given me a chance to explain . . .'

Immediately, Matilda's 'television' alter ego vaporised. Her mother had gone too far and she felt herself ready to snap.

'A chance to explain?' she flung back at her mother. 'I'm eighteen years old! What do you want, a deathbed scene? I mean, how long do you need?'

She kept her eyes fixed on her mother's, yet even so, she felt lost. Though she had spoken the truth, she thought her words still sounded like soap opera dialogue. The whole conversation suddenly struck her as unreal: no matter what she said now, her language would sound contrived, as if it had been voiced by a million discontented teenage girls before. How could she make her mother understand that she really meant it? How could she make her words count?

Charlotte, her face now drawn and pale, sobbed, 'You don't understand . . .'

Matilda felt sick. She wasn't going to start apologising again. All her life she had been saying sorry, thinking of ways to make life easier for her mother, anticipating every problem before it surfaced. Suddenly she resolved she would never fall for her mother's tricks again.

'You're right, I don't understand,' she said, then she turned and started to leave.

It seemed that Charlotte was not ready to let her go, however. Matilda knew her mother – understood the many years' experience she had when it came to twisting the truth. This argument, like all the ones before it, would be a push-over. It would be only a matter of seconds before Charlotte would regain control: she'd begin to build up Matilda's sympathy and then pile on the guilt. In a few seconds Matilda would feel herself succumbing once more to her mother's power and, just as before, she would feel sick with herself for giving in.

Charlotte cleared her throat and, in a voice not much louder than a whisper, begged, 'For once in your life, please, just talk to me . . . tell me what you're thinking . . .'

Matilda hesitated. There was something raw in her mother's tone, something unfamiliar. She had the impression her mother was trying to be genuine. 'Tell me what you're thinking.' The request took Matilda by surprise. Her mother had never before shown so much interest in her. Sure, she collected information about her daughter – enough to ensure that she could control her – but never before had she asked anything that might lead her to better understand her daughter. It was as if, instead of simply firing question after question, she was actually prepared to listen to the reply. Matilda had been given a chance to let her mother into her private, secret world . . . to leave her better informed. She frowned, then, before she could stop herself, the words surfaced and she said, calmly, quietly, 'You're poisonous. I hate you.'

Never had she spoken so truthfully, and never before had she regretted anything so completely. Right before her, in front of her eyes, she saw her mother collapse, her immobile outer shell no disguise for what was taking place within. Tears flowed from Charlotte's eyes and her lips trembled as she looked blankly towards Matilda, seeing nothing but the blur of her daughter's body in front of her.

It was, recalled Matilda, one of the worst moments of her life – seeing her mother cry from pain rather than from a drive for attention chilled her to the bone. She would not take a step towards Charlotte, however; she would not comfort this woman because the sickening truth was that she had meant every word. She did hate her mother – yet the fact was so painful, so unbearable now that it had been spoken aloud, that she felt sick with shame. It was shame that compelled her to add, in a voice that was so clear, so level it surprised her: 'I'm sorry.'

And then she left. She walked away from the house, knowing deep down that she would never return. It was finally over.

Arriving back at the motel, Edwin let them in and sat on the couch, staring ahead like someone lulled into a waiting-room trance. He said nothing, merely sat looking into space, unaware of Matilda's increasing discomfort as the minutes passed by.

Finding herself back in the unit, she suddenly became conscious of several things at once: that she was sharing the motel room with Edwin, that they had not eaten all day and there was no food in the place, that she didn't know where she should put her bags – where she could lay out her things, or which room she would be sleeping in. She was bothered, too, by the return of her headache, a sharp pain at her temples that left her feeling nauseous and sensitive to even the dull light that shone from the bulb above the table. It was time for her to take her pills and for a moment she felt self-conscious about that, too; wondering how she could pull the various bottles and tablets from her bag without arousing Edwin's curiosity. She glanced in his direction and, seeing that he had not moved, decided to simply risk it. She crouched down next to her bag and rummaged around for her medication.

Up until now she hadn't given much thought to how she would 'live' with Edwin over the next few days or weeks. She had been so taken up with the thought of her documentary and his search that the day-to-day arrangements of sharing a space with this man had made little impact on her. But now, standing in the bathroom, swallowing one pill after another, she realised that their lives were joined in a way that extended beyond a working relationship, and that there was clearly some reason for their being brought together. Fate, she murmured in a dramatic voice. Then, raising her eyebrows and grimacing at herself in the mirror, she opened the door and returned to the living room.

Sitting on the couch as Matilda pottered about in the kitchen area, making tea and phoning for a takeaway pizza, I could think of only two things. Neither of them was related to any of the events that had taken place during my visit to Frances's home. I think the shock of seeing those photographs, of discovering so much, had left me so stunned I couldn't concentrate on anything other than small, inconsequential details.

One of those details related to the bizarre story Matilda told me about meeting Jacob while working on a glass-bottomed boat. What, I wanted to know, had attracted her to him? To me, they appeared mismatched – I couldn't begin to understand what she had seen in him. But that was just a passing thought, replaced by one of no more consequence. It related to my childhood. I remember that as a child of four or five I took it upon myself to chase sparrows from the sanatorium's dining room. I regarded it as my personal responsibility to keep the sparrows at bay, much as I kept the invading Japanese at bay, too, I suppose. It was a game played with the utmost concentration and seriousness of intent. Only now do the expressions I saw on the patients' faces make sense. At the time I was conscious only of being the centre of attention and of staging a performance. I was an only child and, as such, gloried in adult attention. I felt special – as if my mere presence enchanted even the most weary of residents. I suppose I was precocious in a way – though that's hardly the first word that springs to mind. I was, I think, typical of many only children; that is to say: indulged.

Every lunchtime I would run from table to table, squawking and giggling in equal measure as I chased sparrows from the hall. I lived in a fantasy world, seeing myself as a Spitfire pilot chasing down the enemy, or sometimes – more frequently in fact – as a hawk swooping on its prey. It didn't occur to me that I was one of only a handful of people in the entire complex capable of running. I never gave any thought to the fact that I was healthy, or normal, and that the other occupants were ill. It's only now that I realise the patients were watching me with a mixture of longing and envy on their faces. Watching me run and swoop reminded them of all the things they had once possessed but now lost. I'm sorry, now, that I didn't understand, but as a five-year-old I simply enjoyed being the centre of attention, and being entrusted with the task of chasing birds.

I think I must have been about seven before I fully understood that I was healthy and that almost everyone else around me was sick. Today, in this age of 'victimless' society, there would be a glib phrase to describe the sanatorium residents. They would be labelled as 'living with TB'. Almost everyone who falls prey to some illness or disability these days is said to be 'living with . . .'

Personally, although I am well aware that the term has been coined to give a positive spin to an unfortunate state, I find the phrase 'living with . . .' somewhat demeaning. To my ears it draws attention away from the fact that people endure great suffering and sometimes face death with courage and dignity. I wonder how my father would have liked to have been labelled? Did he 'live with a broken heart', or die from it? I wish I could ask him.

There is something else I would like to ask him – something that has only just been revealed to me. As I was looking through the pile of photos this evening I saw something even Frances had been unaware of. Clearly depicted in one of the photos – though standing off to one side, behind my mother and her young twin daughters – was my father. My father had known about his wife's other family all along. He *knew*.

SIX

Edwin reached for a slice of pizza, raising its limp triangle to his mouth and taking a bite. He had barely spoken since returning from Frances's house, and yet, despite his silence, he felt wide awake, as if experiencing the aftershocks of some electrical surge that continued to flow through his body. His brain buzzed, and the only way he could keep control of the information that assaulted him from all directions was by concentrating as hard as he could on as little as possible. The pizza slice in his hand, the taste of sweet tomato paste in his mouth, the warmth of the red wine in his glass, the look of concern on Matilda's face.

She had been watching him like a hawk, but for the moment he could think of nothing to say to her. He could not imagine himself talking ever again. If he did, he knew his voice would crack and then his body would follow suit. His body the surface of a frozen puddle stepped on by a curious, playful child: its beautiful clean surface cracking, fracturing and then destroyed, becoming no more than a shallow muddy pool.

And then it dawned on him: he already was that muddy pool. He had been since the moment he recognised his father in that photograph, when he *knew*, finally, that his father had deceived him.

Anger welled up in Edwin as he remembered his father: that kind, quiet man who had stroked his hair and read to him at bedtime, the man who had stood alone listening to the piano tunes that filtered through the sanatorium garden, the expression of loss so deeply lined in his face. That gentle, considerate man, Edwin thought bitterly, had been little more than a liar. The fact that his mother had left suddenly seemed less important: what mattered was the fact that his father – a man for whom Edwin had felt the utmost respect and love – had known all along where she was. That she was alive. All those years, thought Edwin . . . all those years: those birthdays and Christmases when I waited and waited for Jess to return . . . Albert could have taken me to see her. Albert knew where she was and he said nothing.

'Where is that picture taken, do you think?' he had asked Frances, his voice even then beginning to break.

'That one?' replied Frances, taking the photograph from Edwin's hand. 'It's not a very good one of your mother, is it? She's looks very awkward – but maybe that's because Alberta is tugging at her dress. And look at that dress! It's so glamorous, it's like something pulled from a dress-up box. God, she looks uncomfortable – but look at her waist! Twins. She'd given birth to twins, and yet look at her. Her waist is tiny.'

Edwin had looked at his mother's waist and a wave of pain washed over him. 'Twins?' he wanted to protest. 'Not twins. She had three children. I was her child first. She held me in her arms and told me she loved me and I believed her. I had her first!'

Instead, he repeated, 'Do you know where the picture was taken?'

Once more Frances had scrutinised the image, shaking her head and turning the photo in her hand as if expecting to find an inscription on the back. There was nothing. She shook her head and murmured, 'Well, it could be taken at Franz but I don't recognise it – it looks too formal, almost as if it's the botanic gardens somewhere. I wonder if it's Dunedin? Jess went there from time to time – once a year or so – but she often left Beth and Alberta with my mother during those trips. It might be Dunedin, though. Or Hokitika. Thomas was from near Hokitika, originally.'

'Thomas?' It was the first time Edwin had heard the name.

'Thomas. Her husband. He was such a wonderful man.'

Edwin took a sip of his wine and tried to smile at Matilda but his heart felt heavy, weighed down by what he had discovered. He took another mouthful then held out his glass for a top-up. There was still a centimetre of wine in the bottom but he couldn't wait for it to empty before refilling it. He wouldn't get drunk, though – he had no intention of losing control and making a fool of himself. He wasn't the type to swim naked beneath a glass-bottomed boat. He just needed a drink: something to fill the emptiness.

He glanced up and noticed that Matilda was hovering. She had been watching him all day; first through her video recorder and now she was simply watching, anticipating his next move. Like him, she was drinking, but only as a means to fill in time, to make the atmosphere in the room a bit more bearable.

Edwin realised she hadn't asked him any questions since returning to the motel. She had not mentioned the visit to Frances's house but had set about organising dinner, making cups of tea, opening the wine. She was as flustered as he was, Edwin realised. She looked lost, as if she had no idea what to say or do. He had the vaguest sense that she was waiting for him to speak, to help her out of a difficult – or at least awkward – situation, yet he felt little inclined to do so. She had no idea about what had happened. Despite filming it all, she had seen nothing.

'Do you mind if I turn on the radio?'

Edwin was surprised by Matilda's request but he raised no objection. He listened as music filled the room, a smile creeping across his face as the song drew to a close and the radio presenter announced, 'The wonderful voice of Keith Barry with "My Nova Scotia Home".'

Hearing those words, Edwin couldn't help but laugh. And in laughing he suddenly experienced a sensation of lightness, as if some of the weight of the day that had settled so heavily on his shoulders had lifted. 'Keith Barry!' he all but exploded. 'That's it. That's the name I've been looking for!' The sound of his laughter must have shaken Matilda, because she was searching his face as if he was a madman.

Anticipating her question, Edwin responded, 'It's just a song that haunts me from time to time. It's not important.'

Seeing that his explanation had done nothing to counter the look of concern on Matilda's face, he continued, 'I don't like the song, particularly. I was thinking about it the day I came to your house . . . with the photographs.'

'That seems a long time ago,' said Matilda.

Edwin glanced at her and slowly nodded, 'Yes, it does, doesn't it?'

'It seems like things have turned about, somehow,' continued Matilda. 'As if that day was the start of something. Do you believe in signs? Or fate?'

He looked at her, trying to understand what she was hinting at, but he had no idea. 'No,' he said after a moment's thought.

Matilda smiled. 'Me neither. Well, not really. I kind of do.'

Edwin nodded, his eyes resting on Matilda – this strange girl sitting opposite him. 'I don't really believe in fate, I suppose,' he said.

'Not even after a day like today?' asked Matilda. 'I mean, don't you think about why your mother is still alive – how you'll be able to meet her before she . . .' She stopped abruptly and looked down at the table, her eyes focused on her hands, which fluttered slightly, as if blown by a soft breeze.

'Why don't you hate your mother?' she asked.

Silence met the question, causing Matilda to look up.

'After everything she did to you – why don't you hate her?'

Edwin shrugged, unable to respond.

'She's been alive all this time,' Matilda continued, 'and she never came back for you. Why don't you hate her?'

Again, all Edwin could do was shrug. He felt foolish, unable to explain his emotions, his feelings for his mother, which appeared to be frozen in the past. How was it possible, he wondered, to still love a woman who had abandoned him? And yet he did still love her. He loved her as much now as he did when he was a child. His very first memories were intrinsically linked to his mother; his belief that she loved him was so strong he never thought to question it or to imagine a life without her. She had been his life, just as he had thought he was hers. It was an absolute: a fact he didn't need to prove in the same way he didn't need to prove that the earth was round or that the ground would always remain beneath his feet.

He remembered his mother as a gentle, caring, loving woman

– someone who had always been there to comfort him, to hold him or talk to him. She, more than anyone else, had kept him company. She taught him to read and write, to play the piano, to identify the flowers growing in their garden; she was proud of him – she told him so, and although he sensed it was a form of stubborn blindness on his part, he wasn't prepared to discard any of those memories. He had loved her so completely he couldn't erase the thought of her from his life. He sighed.

At that moment he felt like an old man lying awake in a hospital bed during the early hours of the morning. Too ill to return home yet unable to die, all he could do was look at the ceiling and wait. In his mind's eye he saw the man toy with the starched sheets, folding an edge back and forth in his fingers. He saw the man turn his head towards the door as a footstep outside his room caught his attention. He recognised the flicker of hope on the man's face: the thought passing through his head that someone was poised to enter the room – that someone would come in and sit down next to his bed and hold his hand. That there was someone, one person, in the whole world who understood that he needed comforting – and did something about it.

I'm still waiting for her to return, Edwin thought. Then, meeting Matilda's glance, he said, 'I've never heard my mother's side of the story. I can't hate someone I don't understand . . .' His voice faltered and he looked down at his plate, the crust of his pizza a crooked smile leering back at him.

He gulped, heard Matilda respond, 'I think you must be a saint or something.' Then his shoulders shuddered and, his face contorting, he bowed his head, the fingers of his right hand seeking those of his left and gripping them tight.

It was a sunny day, wasn't it, Edwin? Apparently the weather on the coast is better, more settled, in winter than summer. I didn't know that, as I had never been to the West Coast before. The closest I'd ever been was to Lake Hawea. I had no idea the coast was so close. I'd imagined we'd be driving all day, but we were in Haast by eleven, standing in that dairy ordering two cups of coffee, trying not to eavesdrop on the conversation those middle-aged foreign tourists were having.

I say trying not to listen, but really I mean trying not to interfere. They were behind us, standing at the counter reading aloud from a sign attached to the till. 'Customers wearing citronella,' the sign read, 'will not be served.' The man read the words in perfect English, without making a single mistake, but it was clear all the same that he was puzzled because after a short conversation with his partner in what sounded like Dutch, he turned to us and asked, 'What is citronella?' I listened as you described it to him, mentioning as you did its strong citrus smell – a smell that some people find offensive. He nodded as you spoke, waiting for you to finish before responding, 'It is a natural oil?' You nodded, yes, to which he snapped, 'Then it is not effective. I know these things.'

His remark caught me off guard and I laughed, coffee spluttering through my nose and down the front of my T-shirt.

We arrived in Franz around four. The drive up the coast was so beautiful we didn't see any need to hurry. That's what we said, anyway – we hid behind that excuse; it was more convenient than admitting we were nervous. I can only imagine what thoughts were going through your head because as we drew nearer to Franz Josef you became increasingly quiet, lost in thought. It was something of a relief, I imagine, to know that Frances had phoned ahead. It was kind of her to offer to pave the way, especially since she and Beth, Jess's daughter, hadn't kept in touch after Violet's death. Frances is kind, though – I know that now that I've spent more time getting to know her. She's good at organising things, like arranging for us to go to Beth's for lunch. I wonder what they talked about. Edwin, you shrug a lot – did you know that? Whenever you are uncertain, or feel that things are out of your hands, you shrug. You're like a little boy, shrugging your way through a difficult situation.

I felt bad about filming you. I hadn't understood just how intrusive my camera would be. It was all but impossible to ignore, but we tried our best, didn't we? If I'd given it a bit more thought I would never have started on this documentary about you ... but that's the thing, isn't it? If you thought everything through to its possible conclusion you'd never start anything – you'd be too scared. I would, anyway.

SEVEN

It was a beautiful morning. Matilda woke early and stepped outside, taking her cup of tea with her. Edwin was sleeping in the bedroom. It was an arrangement they felt comfortable with: Edwin took the double bed while Matilda had the single divan or couch bed in the motel unit's living room. During the night, if she felt sick or woke in a sweat, she was able to move around without disturbing Edwin. Only once had he seen her reach for her medication, yet, like a gentleman, he had said nothing. He had turned away. It wasn't that he pretended not to see but that he allowed her her privacy.

As she stood, taking in the view, she rested her hand on her waist. It felt soft to the touch. Despite her loss of weight, fat seemed to settle around her midriff, creating a slight roll which she squeezed with her fingers. She didn't like having a thick waist – it made her feel misshapen. Glancing down at her feet she noticed the length of her toenails before shifting her attention to her thin calves, taking in the hairs that grew in sparse, grass-like clumps along her shins. She would shave her legs, get herself sorted out before meeting Edwin's sister. She wanted to look well presented; it was the least she could do. She wouldn't let Edwin down. He had enough on his plate without having to account for her presence.

She scanned the hillside, her eyes settling on a fragment of glacier, barely discernible through a gap in the mist that filled the valley. She knew nothing about glaciers; she had never seen one before. In the past few days she had pieced together snippets of information about Edwin's mother: that she had been employed as a glacier guide, leading small groups of tourists onto the ice so that they could experience the majesty of their surroundings. Edwin had used the word 'majesty' and Matilda had been momentarily taken aback hearing it. Most of the time he talked like her, using the kind of words she would use herself, but every now and again he would slip in a word she had not anticipated: majestic, marvellous, bucolic . . . She took note of them, storing them in the back of her mind, labelling them 'Edwin words'. They were special. Whereas Jacob and friends of her own age fell back on Awesome! Mental! Cool! Sweet!, she found 'Edwin words' to be somehow more gentle, thoughtful . . . intimate.

Her favourite phrase, one she had heard every night since sharing a motel unit with him, was 'Night and bless'. The first time she heard it she had been taken aback. Hearing the words, she had been immediately transported back to childhood – not her own, but the childhood depicted in books. The kind of childhood where a mother sits on the edge of her daughter's bed and tucks the blankets in and rests a moment, looking down at the child's face, smiling or stroking her hair before bending down and kissing her on the forehead. 'Night and bless' might be the last words the child hears as the mother edges slowly towards the door, hesitating for a moment before switching off the bedroom light. Matilda could imagine the little girl lying in bed, glancing up towards the ceiling and feeling shrouded in love, protected and safe, knowing that the hall light was on and that only a few rooms away her mother would be sitting quietly, reading or thinking, waiting impatiently for the morning when she would see her daughter again – when she would wake up full of joy, knowing that everything – the house, their lives, the future – was complete.

Now, as an adult, she found herself anticipating Edwin's good-night. It was like a prayer, or a promise – 'Everything will be all right,' it suggested. 'I will see you in the morning. I will still be here.' A slight smile spread across Matilda's face. Hearing a noise in the room behind her, she turned and saw Edwin. Her smile broadened into a grin. He was awake! It was as if he had just returned after a long absence – he was back.

'Are you sure you're going to be comfortable, dressed like that?'
Matilda looked down at her clothes and shoes, sweeping her hands over her skirt as she did so. It was true, she had got things slightly wrong – dressing for the visit to Edwin's half-sister's house rather than a walk to the glacier. It had been Edwin's idea to spend the morning outdoors. He said it had been years since he had last been in Franz Josef and he would like to walk up to the face of the glacier and would Matilda care to join him? He appeared oblivious to the fact that she was wearing a skirt and high-heeled shoes – the ones she had worn the day of the wedding photos. It was only as they got into the car that he became aware of her appearance, suggesting that it might be a good idea if she changed into something more suited to walking.

'But I wanted to look neat for your sister,' responded Matilda. 'Like a professional . . .' She saw Edwin flinch at the mention of his half-sister and she understood at once that he had been trying to put the visit to the back of his mind; he did not want to think about meeting Beth. During breakfast he had been strangely calm, almost remote, and despite her best attempts to draw him out he had said little. Watching him, she had felt increasingly despondent. His withdrawal, his lack of interaction had drained her . . . She had felt like a public speaker losing the audience's interest a few minutes into an hour-long presentation. She had floundered and all but given up when out of the blue he had suggested walking to the glacier.

'Bring your camera,' he'd added. 'You might get some pretty shots.'

And now, dressed in combat trousers and a hoodie, she was walking beside him, following a well-formed gravel path through the bush as they made their way upriver towards the glacier. Groups of people passed them: tourists from buses that had lined up in the parking area, the drivers slumped in their seats, eyes shut, commanders of empty vessels. As they edged past one another, greetings would be exchanged: 'Morning, great day for it – have a good one!' 'Not far now . . .' Each greeting was accompanied by a smile, as if all the people walking this route were somehow members of the same community, supporters of one another's efforts to 'see the view'.

By the time they reached the lookout point at the edge of the bush, Matilda was exhausted. She could see the glacier, still a kilometre distant at the head of the river flats. Groups of people lined the track ahead, some striding purposefully, overtaking those who moved at a more leisurely pace or who had stopped to take in the view. Resting on a bench, Matilda was aware that Edwin was not even puffing; he had barely noticed the walk and it had certainly not extended him. He set off again and then realised she was not beside him. Momentarily confused, he turned to see her still sitting on the bench.

A look of concern crossed his face as he joined her. 'Are you feeling all right? You look pale.'

Matilda nodded but said nothing, sick with herself for feeling so weak. At times like this she hated herself; hated the fact that her body was so useless – that she found something as simple as walking a few kilometres beyond her reach. She wished she could command her body to work properly, to pull itself together, but there was nothing she could do. There was nothing. It was all so frustrating but, worse than that, it was humiliating. She felt tears well up in the corners of her eyes and, swiping at them with the back of her hand, she said, 'Why don't you go ahead and I'll catch you up.'

A sudden surge of anger hit her and she realised she didn't want Edwin to stay with her. She meant it when she suggested he go on without her. There was no point him being held back by an invalid; he might as well go on ahead and enjoy himself. The look of puzzled concern on his face annoyed her. How dare he? she thought to herself. How dare he? It was all she could do not to push him away but then, just as quickly as her anger had presented itself, it faded, seeping out of her, leaving her calm and empty.

'I came here once when I was a child,' said Edwin, still seated beside her. 'My father took me on holiday – the only holiday we ever had. It was before the sealed road through the Haast was put in ... There was a track, I believe – a bullock track or a gravel road, I'm not sure. Anyway, we approached Franz from the other end, from the north, via Hokitika. I think, if my memory serves me right, the road south may have ended at Franz Josef.'

Matilda looked down at her feet. She felt foolish. Even though she had barely spoken she wanted to apologise to Edwin for feeling so angry – it wasn't his fault. He was such a kind man. For a moment she wondered if she should tell him about her illness, the reason why she was so unfit, but she couldn't. Even thinking about telling him made her throat feel dry.

'We stayed at a hotel,' said Edwin. 'It was very smart but old-fashioned by today's standards. I shared a bed with my father. He was a thin, bony man. He was one of those old-fashioned men with thin wrists and pale, long legs. Up until that point I had never seen him in anything other than a three-piece suit – he was always smartly dressed, even at six in the morning. But on that holiday I saw him in pyjamas. To tell the truth, I found his appearance shocking. He looked old rather than distinguished. My, he was bony. I remember waking during the night and being convinced that there was a skeleton next to me. I must have made a fuss because I recall waking my father and insisting that he turn on the light so I could see for myself that it was him and not a pile of bones lying beside me.'

Edwin stopped talking, turned to Matilda and shrugged. 'There's no point or moral to this story, Matilda. It's just a memory, that's all: my father and me.'

A look of complete bafflement clouded his face and he glanced away, towards the glacier. He shifted in his seat, adjusting his jacket, searching in his pocket for something.

It happened quickly. Without stopping to think, Matilda touched Edwin gently on the shoulder, saying quietly, 'I have to do this, I'm sorry.' And she kissed him.

I don't know how it happened, Matilda, but I think you fell in love with me. That sounds conceited and I'm sorry, but I think that's what happened. Maybe I was just a stand-in for someone else. I didn't ask. I didn't want to know. I was scared.

People don't do it like this any more, but I think you fell in love with me and because of that you wanted to make love. I'm not so vain as to imagine you were sexually attracted to me. Sex had little to do with it. I have had sex with many women in the past but what I experienced, or felt, with you was altogether different.

To tell the truth, Matilda, I don't understand. Had you been sending me some kind of signal, some 'thing' I should have noticed? Had you given any indication of being interested in me? I hate to say this – but if you did, I failed to see the signs. It never even occurred to me to look. I am out of my depth and I don't know how we reached the moment of being in bed together. You asked me if I believed in fate. Or signs. I don't know about you, Matilda, but I'm beginning to think I should believe in miracles.

Nothing prepared me for the sight of your naked body. My God, you were – are – the most beautiful woman in the world. I couldn't breathe. Do you remember? I must have struck you as ridiculous

– this gasping, elderly man in bed next to you. I'll admit it to you: it crossed my mind that you were playing some kind of trick on me; that for some reason you wished to humiliate me ... but it wasn't a trick, was it? It was real. Forty years separate us in age, Matilda, but when you looked at me I didn't feel old. I felt bewildered, yes, but not old.

You insisted I wear a condom. Gosh, what a suggestion! But when I saw your expression – it was a look almost of pain – I complied. You had one in your overnight bag – what a treasure trove! I had no idea women carried so much around with them. I'm sure the condom wasn't intended for my use. Maybe it was still there from when you lived with Jacob. Can you imagine what was going through my head as you rummaged around in your bag for the thing?

We can laugh about it now, but do you recall what happened? You said it didn't matter. You were kind, pretending not to notice as I fumbled to roll it over my penis. Oh, if only you knew, Matilda, how difficult it was ... If I'd been wearing gardening gloves or had my thumbs tied together, I couldn't have made a worse job of it. You took over. I lost my erection. The condom was in position, remember, but my penis had all but disappeared. Have you ever seen one of those tequila bottles with a worm inside? Well, I think I now know how the worm feels!

You smiled at me but said nothing. I could have fallen in love with you for that reason alone. I remember the way you searched me out; you embraced me with every part of your body: your eyes, your lips, your arms ... your legs. You touched me. I felt touched ... enfolded. It was all I could do not to cry. I almost laughed, I felt so light-headed. Have you ever felt like that, Matilda? I felt as if I had been taken out of myself, as if I could rejoice in myself, in you ... in us. Why did you choose me?

I thought my heart would break. Not from joy or sorrow but simply from use.

EIGHT

Beth's house was easy to find. A few kilometres south of Franz Josef, it stood on the edge of a patch of cleared land near Docherty Stream. The grass, Edwin noted as he parked the car, was almost emerald green, several shades lighter than the bush that surrounded the house on three sides. There was something almost primitive about the setting, as if, like wolves threatening a campsite, the encroaching bush had been kept at bay by fires, and the moment the occupants' backs were turned it would begin steadily, defiantly to approach once more.

Looking beyond the For Sale notice by the front gate, Edwin took in the small herd of cows that gazed on the tufted grass, their backs turned against the rain, which fell heavily from a heavy, overcast sky. Seconds after he switched off the windscreen wipers the surroundings slipped from view, to be replaced by spots then torrents of water. Mist slowly formed on the glass as both Edwin and Matilda remained seated, neither one of them making any attempt to open the door. Edwin turned the wipers back on, leaving them on a slow setting so that they swished the water on the screen back and forth in a listless volley.

'It looks deserted,' remarked Edwin after a while. His eyes

fixed on the house before him, he added absently, 'It could do with a paint . . .'

'It reminds me of my place back in Banana,' said Matilda. 'It's got that same abandoned look – like whoever lives there has given up . . .' She fell silent, unaware that Edwin had turned to face her, silently willing her to tell him something else – anything that might detain him from his appointment with Beth.

'You haven't told me much about your childhood,' he said.

'There's nothing much to tell,' replied Matilda, drawing her knees up to her chin as she sat beside him. 'Banana's a bit of a dump, I suppose, full of rednecks and wasters . . . What you'd expect from a place like that.'

Despite the harshness in her voice, Edwin had the strange impression that Matilda wanted to talk more about her life – that she was on the verge of telling him something. He turned away from her, focusing his attention once more on the house, hoping that his apparent detachment might bring her out of herself.

'Small towns are the same wherever you go,' he said. His remark was met with silence and he immediately regretted having made such a gross generalisation. In that instant he recalled the sensation of Matilda's kiss and his body gave an involuntary jerk.

He hadn't understood why she had kissed him, yet, having been kissed by her, he felt certain that something had changed in their relationship. He couldn't make sense of it, however. He wasn't sure what had changed, how it had changed – all he knew was that she had kissed him and now something was different between them. Something had been added to their relationship. Maybe if it had been a playful, spur-of-the-moment gesture he wouldn't have been affected in the same way. But because she had apologised before kissing him – 'I'm sorry, I have to do this' – the kiss itself had been given *weight*; it meant something.

Incredibly, she had seen something in him that she felt the need to respond to. Was that it? he wondered. Surely she wasn't attracted to him – that made even less sense. Just as he had that morning, he found himself again flustered, disconcerted. He glanced at his watch, noted that it was already two o'clock and that they were very late for lunch.

'Matilda,' he began, 'about this morning . . .' His voice trailed off, interrupted by the appearance of a woman standing on the porch in front of the house. Slowly, uncertainly, she raised her hand and waved, signalling them to come inside. She took a step towards them and, automatically, thinking no more of Matilda, Edwin turned off the wipers, opened his door and climbed out of the car.

Despite the rain, they stood for several minutes on the porch, looking out across the paddocks towards the cloud-covered mountains. 'You should have been here earlier,' said Beth. 'It was sunny and the view was glorious.'

Edwin smiled. 'We went for a walk up to the glacier this morning – that's why we're so late, I'm sorry.'

Beth nodded, glancing from Edwin to Matilda, a puzzled frown clouding her face. She sighed, then, indicating the For Sale sign, said, 'It will be hard to leave this place. I've spent my whole life here.' Anticipating Edwin's question she continued, 'I want to be nearer my mother . . .' Suddenly aware of what she had said, she corrected herself, saying, 'our mother . . .' before adding, 'she moved back to Central. She was determined to end her days there. She can be very stubborn when she sets her mind to something . . .' Her gaze rested once more on Edwin and he shifted self-consciously, aware that she was searching for something, perhaps some indication of a family likeness – which, after all, was what he had been doing too.

'The real estate agent told me she had hundreds of buyers lined up for "authentic" properties like this one,' Beth continued, the lightness of her voice at odds with the intensity of her gaze, which all but drilled a hole into Edwin. She laughed suddenly as if finding something deeply ironic in her previous statement. 'I think buyers have been put off by just how "authentic" the property is! There's something about living in a house with an outside toilet that seems to make overseas buyers nervous; I think they quickly realise that wanting a house "just like this one" means they'd prefer someone else's . . .' She laughed again, openly this time, and Edwin recognised something mischievous in her expression. Facing Edwin, Beth held his glance and smiled. 'It's hard to believe, isn't it? You're here . . . and . . .' She glanced at Matilda. 'And your friend too.'

Remaining on the porch, they chatted on, small talk tossed back and forth between them as they continued to weigh each other up. It wasn't long, however, before they managed to begin to feel at ease, their conversation becoming less awkward with the passing of each minute. Listening to Beth, Edwin forgot his surroundings and concentrated solely on what his half-sister had to say. Any mention of his mother was precious; he felt as if he was being allowed access to the most important information of his life, words that had the power to define his place in the world. He hung on to every word, oblivious to the fact that Beth seemed unaware of the weight he was giving to her remarks.

They were halfway through lunch, a meal of cold meat and

potato salad, when Beth suddenly put down her fork, dropping her head into her hands. The room, Edwin noticed, became deathly quiet, save for the sound made by a pale blue budgie that pecked and nibbled at a plastic-framed mirror in its cage. Feeling uncomfortable and unsure of what to say, Edwin glanced around the room and noticed, with a shock, that it was decorated with the same bamboo wallpaper as his own living room. Hanging on the walls were several photographs: some of mountain scenes, others of people in various foreign countries and one of a plump young woman in a long black evening gown. He turned to look at the rest of the room, taking in the threadbare carpet and the brown vinyl couch covered with fraying tweed cushions. Although the furnishings were worn, shabby even, the room was immaculately clean. Every surface, every object, gleamed – polished and positioned so neatly that it appeared almost as if nothing had ever been rearranged or moved.

Edwin glanced at Matilda. As usual, she had said little since arriving, taking her place on a chair a few feet away, her lunch sitting untouched on a fold-out metal television tray as she filmed. Her face, Edwin noticed, was pale and as he watched she looked up, raising her hand to her forehead several times before turning her attention back to her camera. Noticing that she had been observed by Edwin, she frowned, then asked if she could have a glass of water. Her voice, cutting as it did through the stillness of the room, caught Beth's attention. Looking up, she glanced around, her eyes glistening from tears.

Fixing her gaze on Edwin's she cleared her throat. 'I never heard my parents argue,' she said. 'As a child I always had the impression that they loved each other completely – that deep down they had no need for anyone else to make their lives complete. My sister and I were "accidents" of course – Jess gave birth to us when she was in her forties and I used to have the impression that she thought we would somehow come between her and my father. Despite being very independent, she was also somewhat possessive; jealous, I suppose.

'But my father was a very generous man – he was one of those people who could make room for anyone . . .' Beth wiped her cheek with the back of her hand. 'Once, when I was still quite young, I overheard my parents talking. They weren't arguing, but there was something in my father's tone that stopped me in my tracks. It was unfamiliar – not angry, but firm. It caught my attention and I listened . . . eavesdropped.'

She fell quiet, twisting her wedding band round and round her finger. It was several moments before she took up her story again, and she spoke quietly, as if recalling events for the first time. 'I heard my father say, "He's your son, Jess. You've every right to see him." And I remember my mother replying, "I have no right – not now." I'm pretty certain,' said Beth, 'that those were my mother's words, and then my father said something like, "Albert would never stop you, you know that."'

Edwin flinched at the mention of his father but said nothing, waiting for Beth to finish.

'I didn't know who or what my parents were talking about but I remember this: from that day on I always had a feeling that I had done something wrong. I felt guilty about something – though I didn't know what it was. I formed an idea that out there, somewhere . . .' she said, making a sweeping gesture with her hand, 'was a boy, a child like me, locked away or something, you know, like a stray animal locked up in the pound. I felt guilty . . . that it was my fault the boy wasn't with his parents . . .'

Tears welled up in Beth's eyes and Edwin felt his heart lurch. Leaning towards her, he said, 'It wasn't your fault. It had nothing to do with us.'

'But I felt so guilty,' countered Beth. 'Why had they wanted me and not the boy?'

'Beth,' said Edwin, gently, 'I would have been a young man when you heard that conversation. I must have been in my twenties – I wasn't a child.'

'But I didn't know that!' cried Beth. 'I didn't know anything until recently. No one told me . . . it was all so secret. No one said anything and I never tried to find out. Don't you see? I did nothing – I pretended not to know!'

Edwin glanced helplessly from Beth to Matilda but could think of nothing more to say to ease Beth's distress. He couldn't repair the past. He wanted desperately to comfort her but the only words that sprang to mind were the ones he had already used: 'It wasn't our fault.'

He sat quietly, feeling miserable and uncertain. It seemed to him that too much damage had been caused, that too many people had been hurt – people he hadn't even known existed until recently. It would have been wiser not to have begun this search in the first place. Upsetting so many people achieved nothing. He should have left things as they were.

He glanced towards the window, his attention caught by a tui perched on a flax bush. He kept his eyes focused on its glossy green-black feathers, the white tuft below its neck, watching it until it took flight, disappearing into the dense bush, which seemed closer now than it had before.

Turning back to the room he caught sight of Matilda and gasped. She was pale, beads of sweat formed on her forehead.

Forgetting everything else, Edwin rushed to her side and helped her to the couch, where he sat with her, her head resting in his lap. He could feel the heat of her body through his clothing and a wave of panic went through him. His first thought was that she was dying but, seeing her smile back at him, he began to relax a little, tilting a glass of water Beth passed him, so that Matilda might take small sips. His heart still beating fast, he asked, 'Are you all right?' to which Matilda responded with a nod, reassuring him that there was no need to fuss – she was just a little tired and could do with a rest. She asked Beth for her bag and rummaged for some pills, which she swallowed, explaining that they would soon take effect. She'd be better soon.

Still feeling anxious, Edwin helped her down the hall to a bedroom offered by Beth.

'It's my daughter's room,' she explained. 'The bed's made up. You'll be quiet there.'

Alone with Matilda, Edwin sat on the edge of the bed, scared to leave her in case something – he didn't know what – happened. Despite her protestations that she would be fine, his stomach lurched, and he could not help searching her face for signs of pain or a worsening condition. Realising how little he knew about illnesses, he trawled through his memory for the information contained in brochures he had picked up and read while waiting in Dr Aubrey's surgery. He remembered one recommending immunisation against the flu, a pink brochure promoting breast self-examination, another for the treatment of headlice and one more that contained information about meningitis. His mind skating, he tried to recall the symptoms: fever, blotchy skin . . . a stiff neck. Fearful that Matilda might have contracted the disease, he began to quiz her gently about how she felt. As he listed each symptom of meningitis she shook her head, insisting she was all right, that she would be fine with rest. Edwin was not convinced. Placing his hand on her forehead he asked, 'What about your neck? Does it feel stiff?' To his horror, Matilda laughed, responding that her neck was fine and that he should stop fussing.

To his surprise, Edwin felt cross with her, but before he could say any more she repeated that she was fine and told him to return to Beth. She would call if her neck started seizing up. Edwin knew he was being teased and he began to relax but he stayed put, refusing to move until after Matilda closed her eyes and he sensed she was asleep.

He remained on her bed a few minutes longer, just looking at her, taking in her face, her fine features, her mouth that appeared to be forming words even as she slept. He smiled at her and gently ran his hand over her forehead, the way his father had soothed him whenever he had been in bed, poorly, as a child. He allowed his palm to rest on her head and he felt a desire to stay with her, to watch over her. He touched her hair, feeling the short, soft strands in his fingertips, and he wished he could just take her in his arms and hold her. He wanted to do something for her instead of feeling so helpless all the time. She looked so peaceful, so beautiful. He bent and kissed her lightly on the forehead, then, standing slowly, crept from the room.

Edwin returned to the living room and stood quietly watching as Beth put a match to the fire.

'Is she sleeping?' asked Beth without turning from the fireplace.

'Yes,' replied Edwin.

'Is she often like this? She's very thin and pale,' said Beth, turning now and wiping her hands over her trousers.

'I've seen her take pills – quite a few pills,' said Edwin by way of reply, 'but I don't know what's wrong.'

Beth smiled and gestured to Edwin to take a seat by the fire. 'I'm sure she'll tell you when the time is right. Girls are always a bit proud and tight-lipped – they like their privacy. Don't worry, it will be fine.'

They talked off and on throughout the afternoon, their conversation punctuated by long silences that filled the room but drew them closer, nevertheless. Beth's curiosity about Edwin's life was matched by a willingness to openly discuss her own. She spoke of both her mother and father, her twin sister, Alberta, and her daughter, Maeve, who was away at boarding school in Christchurch.

'I didn't want her to go,' she said simply, 'but she's showing real promise as a singer. She intends to perform opera and, according to her voice coach, she has a good chance of making it.' Turning to the wall, she gestured towards the photograph of the plump girl in an evening dress. 'That's her. I miss her so much – she's such a dag.'

Edwin laughed, then, pointing to another photo, he asked, 'Who's that?'

Beth answered without looking. 'My partner, Tim.' Aware that Edwin was looking at her wedding band, she added, 'We're not married – not in a legal sense. He's a mountaineer – works for a guiding company so he's away a lot. At the moment he's in Tibet. I'm almost the opposite – I've never left the country. I work at the hotel and earn a bit more money giving piano lessons. I also look after the house – until it sells, if it sells. That's all the world I need. I'm happy.'

Edwin nodded, and felt no desire to ask for more details. It seemed to him it wasn't necessary. They didn't have to tell each other everything – not during this first meeting. If things went well, they could get to know each other over time, rather than through one extended session.

They sat quietly, watching the flames flicker and create shadows in the darkening room. Light was fading; it would be dark soon, but neither of them gave any indication of the visit nearing an end. His gaze fixed on a piece of damp wood that hissed and steamed as it burned, Edwin jumped when Beth's voice broke through his thoughts.

'Albert was your father's name, wasn't it?' she asked, her voice barely audible. 'I would have liked to meet him . . . What was he like?'

Edwin frowned, puzzled by Beth's remark, the fact that she seemed not to know his father, despite having been photographed standing next to him. Never before had Edwin spoken ill of his father, but his recent discovery had changed things.

'He was not the man I thought he was. He lied to me and now he's dead, so I won't have the chance to find out why . . .'

Silence descended, then, remembering that he had the photo given him by Frances, Edwin pulled it from his pocket, placing it on the table between him and Beth.

She glanced at it, smiling. 'There's me,' she said, pointing to one of the girls, 'Alberta,' she said, pointing to an identically dressed girl, 'Uncle Charles . . .' she continued, indicating Edwin's father, 'and Jess of course.' She took the photograph in her hands, looking carefully at the image. 'I remember that day.' She smiled. 'We were in Invercargill. My father's sister, my Aunt Ellen, lived there – still does, she's in her nineties now. We used to visit once or twice a year.'

Edwin stared at the photo, as if perhaps he had been mistaken and it wasn't his father's face but that of some 'Uncle Charles'. He felt confused, unsure of what to say.

'Uncle Charles?' he began slowly. 'Was he your father's brother? Your uncle?' He paused as the consequences of his remark sank in. He prayed it wasn't true. With all his heart he prayed that his father was not related to his mother's second husband. She couldn't have married a member of Albert's family, some brother he had never heard of – that would be too cruel.

Suddenly Edwin just wanted all the secrets to end. He realised he'd had enough and he really didn't want to hear that the circle of silence was even larger than he had imagined. Please, he thought to himself, please don't let them be related. The seconds ticked by, moving slowly as he waited for Beth's reply.

'No,' said Beth, 'we just called him Uncle. He was a friend of my mother's, that's all.'

Edwin sighed, relief sweeping through him, causing tears to well in his eyes. Unaware that Beth was watching him, he turned back to the photograph, his eyes resting on his father's face.

'Charles,' said Beth, 'used to visit once or twice a year after my father passed on. He was a very kind man, quiet. He was shy – not like my father, and gentle – a lot like you, I suspect.' She smiled. 'He helped us out from time to time. He paid for Alberta's education – so she could train to be a pharmacist . . . she lives in Kaitaia . . . and he paid for my piano. He was always offering to help. I had the impression he was in love with my mother, that deep down he was hoping that if he waited long enough she would marry him.'

Beth glanced towards the door that opened into the hall and fell silent. A minute passed before either one of them spoke, then, her voice barely above a whisper, Beth said, 'Charles is your father, isn't he? That man in the photograph, the one I've been calling Charles, is really Albert, isn't he? You look exactly like him.'

Tears flowing down his cheeks now, it was all Edwin could do to mutter, 'Frances said I look exactly like my mother.'

Beth smiled and leaned forward, taking Edwin's hand gently in her own. 'I believe your father was a good man, Edwin. He had to be, to do what he did . . .'

Giving in to his emotions, Edwin rested his head in his hands and wept. He felt engulfed by the sorrow that pounded his slumped body. He was embarrassed, but he could not stop. Each time his tears dwindled, he would remember a word or a gesture of one of his parents and the tears would begin to flow once more, sobs choking him as he searched helplessly for a dry corner on his handkerchief. Finally he rose and went outside to the porch, where he stood watching sheets of rain sweep across the dark garden before him. Engrossed by the shadows, he was suddenly aware that behind him a light had been turned on. A square of grass was illuminated bright green and the rain, as it fell, was captured by the light, glittering like small fish caught in a net.

As Edwin stood looking into the emptiness he heard music. From the house came the sound of a piano, a low, sad melody that mingled with the rain and fell in languid curtains. The music calmed him. He listened with his whole body and his mind wandered back over the years, coming to rest on an image of a thin but well-dressed man standing on the edge of a large, well-kept lawn as, behind him, the sound of a waltz drifted softly around his solitary frame.

Yesterday, Edwin, you sat with me in the bedroom at Beth's house. You stayed with me a long time; I could feel the weight of your body pressing down on the edge of the bed. Even though I was awake, I shut my eyes and it was then I realised I knew your face without looking at it. I don't mean I could describe your face: that your eyes are blue, or your hair grey . . . what I mean is that I knew your face. I could recall everything about the way you look: your expression, even the way you bite your lip sometimes when you're thinking – yet I have no recollection of having memorised these things. When I close my eyes I can bring you to mind, and seeing you fills me with a sense of peace. I feel reassured and as if I'm right to trust you.

As soon as I heard you leave the room I opened my eyes and looked around the room. I knew it belonged to Beth's daughter. Like the rest of the house it was very tidy but somehow sparse. Yet, unlike the minimalist bedroom of my first home, in Auckland, this room had character. It was hard to pinpoint exactly what Beth's room had that my own didn't but then I realised it came down to a sensation as much as anything. The room felt lived in, loved – it had a good feeling.

None of the things on the dressing table, for example, appeared particularly expensive or 'designer'. Beside a photograph of a man standing beside a hairy cow, which I took to be a yak, was a doll-thing made from driftwood. Two pieces of paua the size of buttons had been attached to its moon face for eyes, and it had dried seaweed for hair. It was the type of doll my mother might have bought from an *objet* shop in Devonport or Parnell, yet I felt sure this doll was homemade. That it had been made by the man in the photograph for his daughter. I had the impression he had walked the length of a nearby beach and collected the bits and pieces to make the doll and then, with the girl looking over his shoulder, instructing him, he had selected each piece and attached it with string or glue to the driftwood body. The doll had been made by someone who liked making things for his child. I might be wrong of course, but I doubt it.

The sheets on the bed were clean. Not only were they freshly laundered but they were ironed. The top sheet was folded back over the edge of the blanket and the whole bed had a tucked-in feeling about it. Beth had insisted that I get into the bed, under the covers. My own mother would never have allowed a visitor to do that. I can imagine her thinking to herself, She can lie on the bed but not in it because then I'll have to change the sheets and I can't be bothered doing that for someone who is just a little tired. That's how my mother would have approached a situation like this. She wasn't generous. She could spend money but she wasn't generous. But listening to Beth, I had the feeling she wouldn't even think about the bed – she'd be too concerned with the sick visitor to worry about the bed.

The room belonged to Beth's daughter. It had been kept for her. Not 'maintained' for her, the way a room in a historic house might be, but 'kept'. I could imagine Maeve walking in at any minute, plonking herself down on the bed and then smiling, glad to be home. She'd look at the bed, the clean sheets, and she'd feel happy, wanted, and she'd go and thank her mother for being so kind, so thoughtful – adding that it wasn't necessary, that she could have made her own bed. I could imagine her putting her arms around her mother and embracing her, and I could imagine her mother coming back into the room with her daughter just because she wanted to watch her daughter unpack her bags – she'd want to stay close. I could even imagine the mother grabbing the daughter's dirty laundry, despite the daughter's protest that she could do it herself. The daughter would know that the mother was happy to do her washing and she'd let her do it because she understood that her mother wanted to spoil her. And the mother wanted to show her love for her daughter because, more than anything, she did love her daughter. She loved her daughter, she was proud of her daughter and she forgave her daughter for any mistakes or remarks she might have made in her young life. Nothing could come between them because they loved each other.

If I went home, Edwin, what would happen? Would it just be a waste of time or is it worth one last try?

NINE

It had been Matilda's idea to have what she called a 'rest day'.

'If it's all right with you,' she had suggested to Edwin, 'I'd like to visit Lake Matheson and maybe just muck around, have a bit of a break . . . just take things easy?'

Though it was true she felt tired, she was conscious of the fact that Edwin appeared even worse than she felt. He looked completely drained. When he had wandered out of his bedroom and into the living area of the unit that morning he had barely been able to summon up the energy to say 'Good morning'. Taking a slice of white toast and a glass of brightly coloured orange juice from the tray that had been delivered to their unit by a pregnant girl of only fifteen or sixteen, he had sat down at the table and begun to chew slowly before noticing that his toast had neither butter nor honey spread on it. It wasn't until the toast gave way in his mouth, cracking and crumbling into large, dehydrated shards, that he looked up, searching the room absently before allowing his gaze to fall on Matilda, who was perched on the divan, watching him.

'Good morning,' he said, forgetting he had already greeted her. Then running his hand over the grey stubble that covered his chin, he had stood up and wandered into the bathroom, where, through the thin walls, Matilda could hear him simultaneously running the shower and flushing the toilet.

Matilda switched on the television, skimming back and forth through the channels until she settled on the news. Normally she never watched television, but the morning had such a hungover feel to it that she welcomed the opportunity to lie back on her bed and draw the covers around her as she waited for Edwin to reappear. She was aware that her attention was focused not so much on what she was watching but on what she could hear. Having spent some time now in Edwin's company, she had become familiar with his morning routine. The way he shuffled around the bathroom as he cleaned his teeth and shaved. He didn't stand still and she wondered what it was he did, or looked at, as he went through his ablutions.

She knew two things he *didn't* do: he never picked up the bathmat, which was crumpled on the floor when she entered the bathroom each morning; nor did he ever open the window to air out the room. This last fact puzzled her. How, she wondered, did he manage to shave when the mirror was so misted it was impossible to see any reflection? She thought that if she was ever to live with him, share a house with him, both these things had the potential to get on her nerves. Her thoughts drifting from one scenario to another, she imagined what else might irritate her with time. In general, he struck her as an organised person but with a tendency to procrastinate. There was also something *so Edwin* about the way he had come across that image of his mother in that magazine. She couldn't imagine anyone else even picking up a Chinese magazine – unless they could read it. Yet for some reason she knew that Edwin would not *not* pick it up.

Only Edwin could do that – find a photograph of his mother completely by chance – and then deny the existence of fate. And the way he had decided to visit her in Ranfurly and deliver the wedding photographs when anyone else would have realised she didn't want them. It was as if, she mused, he was some kind of accidental romantic. That, and lonely.

Hearing the word 'tuberculosis' on the television she turned her attention back to the screen, catching an item about the outbreak of the disease in a school up north. She remembered being tested for TB. She recalled sitting in a sparsely decorated room, waiting and slowly becoming aware, as she waited, that she was the only white person. Everyone else was either Aboriginal or Asian. She was called into the small consulting room, divided from the main area only by a heavy curtain. The woman doing the test had looked up and smiled at her as she entered. Although Matilda would never know for sure, she had the impression the woman's expression was one almost of relief, as if she saw in Matilda *a person like herself.* That is, an *Australian.* A European. Matilda could see the woman thinking to herself, At last, here is someone who will understand, who will not be difficult. She won't be any trouble . . .'

And then, before Matilda's eyes, the woman had glanced down at her notes and in a fraction of a second her expression had faltered. It had been almost imperceptible, a slight flicker, but when the woman looked up there was no longer any warmth in her expression; the welcome had been withdrawn and she had spoken sharply, instructing Matilda to pull up her sleeve. The test itself had taken only a few seconds but the woman had spent almost a minute beforehand squeezing her hands into two pairs of gloves and afterwards, as she informed Matilda that she had to return in a few days' time to have the test 'read', she had spoken severely, as if she knew Matilda would not return, because people like her never did.

Later, Matilda found out that few HIV patients in her part of Queensland attended public clinics, preferring private, HIV-friendly clinics instead. But she had been grateful for her experience. It had brought her face to face with what her illness *meant*.

From that day on she vowed to continue to attend public clinics and, no matter what, she would always stand her ground. She would not be judged.

Today, she thought, as she waited for Edwin to come out of the bathroom, she would tell him. The night she had whispered to him about her disease didn't count. After all, he had been asleep. That night had been theatre. Today, however, she would tell him, and in telling him she would know, instantly, what kind of man he was. His eyes would give him away.

They arrived at Lake Matheson early, before the first tourist bus. The mist that had obscured the mountain peaks appeared to be lifting but, given the forecast, it was just as likely the rain would come back. They were planning to leave the next day and return to Alexandra. They planned to reunite with Beth and visit Edwin's mother at the rest-home. It had been Beth's idea for her to join them. She had explained that her mother was getting on, that she was sometimes a little muddled and it might be less confusing if she was with them.

'I won't get in your way,' she had assured Edwin, 'but I think I should be there. I always visit on a Saturday anyway. It's our little routine.'

Edwin had thanked Beth and then apologised for disrupting her life. His apology had embarrassed Beth, who had quickly brushed it aside, saying it was the least she could do, and she was only sorry that she couldn't do more. As she spoke, Matilda detected an expression of shame on Beth's face. It struck her that the guilt Beth had spoken of during their first meeting was still present, and that it might take many more meetings with Edwin before she could rid herself of it completely.

Sitting at a table in the Lake Matheson café, lingering over a second pot of tea, Edwin and Matilda had been talking quietly when the door of the café had swung open, revealing a couple in their mid-thirties. The man was grinning, a smile bisecting his face. Glancing around the café and seeing that it was all but empty, he immediately advanced on Edwin and Matilda, extending his hand as he announced, 'Shake hands with the luckiest man in the world!' Taken aback, Edwin proffered his hand, barely aware that the woman beside the grinning man was trying to guide her companion away, protesting as she did. 'Shush, Dean, leave them alone . . . They don't want to hear that.'

'Why not?' countered the man. 'It's true, isn't it? Besides, if you can't tell the world you're lucky when it's your honeymoon . . .'

He grabbed his companion around the waist and gave her a twirl. 'And this beautiful woman,' he said, addressing both staff and customers, 'is my wife, Jane. Jane!' he continued, kissing her. 'My wife!'

The woman, Jane, blushed deeply and mouthed an apology to Edwin as she manoeuvred her husband to a vacant table towards the back of the café.

Edwin's gaze rested on the couple as they walked away. They looked so happy. Before he could stop himself he suddenly said, 'They'll last.'

Matilda looked in the couple's direction, confused. 'Sorry? What was that?'

Edwin blushed. 'Oh,' he said, as if only just now aware of what he had said, 'I used to think I could tell which marriages would last . . . it was something I used to talk to my doctor about.'

'Your doctor?' responded Matilda, unsure of what Edwin was getting at. 'You mean you have some kind of condition? A marriage-predicting condition?' She smiled, waiting for Edwin to respond.

Appearing flustered, he shrugged. 'I spent a lot of time taking wedding portraits – I guess it was intuition . . .'

Her expression suddenly serious, Matilda asked, 'And my marriage to Jacob – did you think that would last?'

Edwin sighed. He felt trapped. Shifting uncomfortably in his seat he looked down at his plate, prodding a piece of boysenberry muffin with his knife, tapping it gently around his plate. 'It doesn't matter what I thought,' he said after a while.

'Come on,' said Matilda, leaning towards him. 'I'm curious. Tell me what you thought.'

The corners of Edwin's mouth turned down but, knowing he could not escape, he answered, finally, 'No, I didn't think it would last.'

A silence greeted his remark and he looked down at his plate once more, wishing the moment would pass, that they could rewind time, maybe returning to the instant when the newly wedded couple had arrived in the café. Instead, he glanced up at Matilda and his heart sank. Her eyes glistened and, although her mouth appeared set in some kind of expression of non-response, he could see she was hurt.

She looked past him, towards the door of the café, as she finally said, 'You're right. It wouldn't have lasted, but probably not for the reason you imagine.'

'I don't have any thoughts on your relationship,' said Edwin quickly. 'I'm sure your marriage would have worked out . . .'

Matilda shook her head, a sad smile spreading across her face. 'Edwin,' she said, 'I was going to tell you this some time today . . .' Her voice faded into silence. A few seconds passed and then, unexpectedly, her voice jerked back into life, like a radio retuned to a channel. 'Jacob wanted to have children.'

Edwin nodded, though he was unsure of where the conversation was leading.

'I didn't . . .' continued Matilda.

Feeling on safer ground, Edwin broke in. 'You're young, Matilda. Who knows what might happen in the future.'

Matilda laughed, the sound so hollow and cold that it took Edwin aback. He found himself staring at his companion as if expecting to see someone else in her chair.

'No,' she said, 'you've got it wrong. You don't understand.'

Edwin shrugged helplessly, caught himself doing it and shrugged again, apologetically.

'He didn't leave me because I don't want children, he left me because I can't have children.'

Bewildered by Matilda's forthrightness, it was all Edwin could do to nod.

'I'm HIV positive, Edwin.'

Edwin felt the air rush out of him. His stomach lurched and before he could think he had leant forward to take Matilda's hand. Missing, he caught her sleeve, gripping it awkwardly in his fingers, jerking her arm towards him.

Matilda smiled. Her face suddenly relaxed a little and she held Edwin's gaze in her own.

'I can't have children,' she continued, 'not because I'm HIV positive but because I got badly damaged in the process of contracting the disease.'

Edwin was confused. He had the feeling Matilda was probably making perfect sense, but not to him.

'Who hurt you?' he wanted to yell, a sense of outrage taking hold. He stiffened, a mixture of anger and disbelief rising to the surface. 'But that's not right! You can't be hurt – you're too good . . . It's not right . . .'

His words, he realised, were meaningless. But there was nothing he could say. There needed to be some other language for moments like these. He looked at Matilda, who seemed to be engrossed in some private memory, and he felt helpless. What had happened to her? How could anyone hurt her?

Laughter erupted from the table behind them. The sound caught Edwin's attention and despite himself he listened as the man's voice rang out: 'Are you calling me desperate?' Laughter flowed from the man as he carried on. 'I'm no more desperate than you! You're the one who answered the ad, remember?' As had happened before, the woman's soft voice responded with a long 'Shush, Dean. Quiet.'

The man laughed once more. 'Touchy, aren't you?' He paused for an instant, before adding in a loud, clear voice: 'Didn't you get enough sleep last night? Did something keep you up?' The man clapped his hands playfully, as if enjoying a particularly funny joke.

The sound caught in Edwin's body; he had the overwhelming desire to walk across to the laughing imbecile and make him shut up. How could he laugh at a time like this? How dare he? The very idea struck him as obscene. Glancing back to Matilda, he realised she had been listening too, but she was smiling.

'They'll last,' she nodded. Then, catching Edwin's eye, she frowned, the smile leaving her face. 'I'm sorry,' she said. 'It can come as a bit of a shock at first.'

Edwin held her gaze and realised, in that moment, that he didn't want her to finish her documentary and then disappear out of his life. He looked at Matilda, saw that she was watching him, and he decided she was the only person in the world he really *cared* about. Surprised by the strength of his feelings, he continued to focus on Matilda, his thoughts on her future – perhaps even their future. His recent obsession with memories of his childhood and his mother faded into the background as he continued to gaze at Matilda who was now looking down at her plate, smiling yet self-conscious at the sudden attention.

Edwin suddenly felt disconcerted, foolish. Of course Matilda wouldn't share his feelings. It was hardly likely that a woman of twenty-two would want to be with him. He stood up and extended his hand, asking Matilda if she would like to join him for a walk around the lake. His gesture was so formal, so old-fashioned that he knew it had caught the attention of the laughing man watching from the other table. Shooting a glance across the room, Edwin met the man's eye and frowned. Whatever happened between him and Matilda, he thought, was no one's business. In a world that, by rights, should be begging Matilda for forgiveness, he felt no need for approval.

Later, hours later, Edwin and Matilda had gone to bed together. Neither of them could remember exactly how it happened. There was a sense that they had drifted into bed; that without anything being said they had found each other and that, having completed their search, they had lain down to rest.

PART FOUR

jess

I haven't seen you since you were seven. That's when I left. I wonder if you remember that day? You were excited because I had said you could go to Ranfurly with the gardener. He was a nice young man, cheerful – the type of man who always smiled. Despite what he had been through in the war, he was completely untroubled by life: an optimist. I recall his name. Samuel.

Your father didn't know I was leaving. He had no idea. He found out an hour before I left and he begged me to stay – but I couldn't, Edwin. I couldn't. Your father didn't find out about Thomas until later. At the time, I couldn't tell him I was leaving him for another man. Perhaps I should have. Maybe it would have simplified things, had he known the truth.

I had to leave you, Edwin. I couldn't take you away from your father. He loved you with all his heart; it would have broken in two had I taken you with me. The truth is, Edwin, he loved you more than I did. I wish that weren't so but it is. I'm sorry.

I made your father promise to tell you I had died. I thought it would be better that way. That, in time, your memory of me would fade and you would just get on with your life. I knew your father would never remarry and I was sorry about that, too. Your father begged me to let him tell you the truth. He said he couldn't keep his son from his mother – it wasn't right – but I made him swear not to tell you. I didn't want you to wait for me when there was no hope of my ever returning. To keep you hoping would be cruel. I imagine your father never did tell you the truth. I have not seen you since the day I left, and that was a long, long time ago.

Today someone from a tourist magazine came and took my photograph. I refused to take part at first but I was told the article was going to appear in a Chinese-language magazine, a general-interest magazine for Chinese New Zealanders. The article will not be translated into English, I am told. You're probably wondering, like I did, why they wanted a photograph of me in the first place. I don't know. It's a feature about Franz Josef, about the community here, the people who live and work here. I used to be a glacier guide. I am told I was the first woman to be employed by a guiding company but I don't think that's true. In any case, it's not important.

As they were taking my photograph I began to think about you. All around me tourists were taking photographs and making recordings on little video camera things – and I began to think about you. I still picture you as a child of seven but I find it hard to remember your face. I didn't take any photographs of you with me when I left. I think if I had taken a photo I wouldn't have been able to look at it – it would have been too painful. I did love you, but not enough; there was someone else I loved more.

Thomas was my love. I met him at the sanatorium. He was not much older than me. Your father, by contrast, was my senior by almost twenty years – that was quite an age gap, even back then, when half the men were away at war and women took what they could get. As you know, your father had had tuberculosis as a child – that was why he was a doctor and not a soldier. Thomas, on the other hand, had been a soldier. The sanatorium, you remember, was full of ex-servicemen. Your friend Samuel had fought in the war, and so had many of the other men. Nurses were in short supply. I don't know if you know this but preference was always given to patients who could provide their own nurse.

I was never a fully trained nurse. I began my training but I never took the final exams. In fact, to tell you the truth, the sight of so much suffering turned my stomach. I could barely bring myself to collect the sputum mugs. They smelt of Lysol but that did little to disguise the contents. It was the task of the night nurse to collect the mugs and take them to the sputum room, where the contents would be examined for blood and measured. Even now I feel queasy just thinking about it.

Your father caught sight of me once as I was standing outside the room retching, and from that day on he always made some excuse to wander into the sputum room on the nights I was on duty. He sensed my squeamishness and took over, and that's how he seduced me – through kindness. He took care of me, anticipated my needs, my worries – he wanted to make me feel better. Your father, Edwin, was one of the best men who ever walked on this earth. Never forget that. I was very fond of him and I've always regretted the fact that I hurt him so.

Thomas was a patient at the sanatorium for two years and, during that time, I found myself falling in love with him. You were five when Thomas arrived. He had a playful sense of humour. He used to drop crumbs for the sparrows in the dining hall. There was a time, Edwin, when you used to take a great deal of pleasure in chasing sparrows from the hall. It was a game you used to play. You were such a lonely child and the patients would feel sorry for you. Knowing how much you enjoyed your game, some of them would drop crumbs for the birds – that way, there would always be sparrows in the hall when you came in at dinner time. Thomas, who was one of the youngest residents, dropped more crumbs than anyone else. I think you reminded him of what it was to be fit and healthy. He never questioned my decision to leave you behind, though I know he was very fond of you and would have liked to take you with us.

I loved Thomas with a passion that verged on madness. I was so in love with him I was unable to think clearly. Nothing mattered as much as being with him. Every part of my body sought him out, yearned for him ... needed him. I don't know how we choose the ones we love – they choose us, don't they? Thomas and I belonged together ... I can't explain it any more clearly than that. Maybe you know the kind of love I mean? You're an adult now; it's possible you know what I'm talking about.

My love for Thomas grew each day – right up until the day he was taken from me. He drowned. He was a fisherman. I thought I would die from grief. I was in my forties and had twin girls and all I wanted was for my life to end. I would have killed myself if it hadn't been for your father. He had tracked me down years before, when you were still a boy, but from the time of Thomas's death he used to visit once or twice a year. He sent me money, ensured that we never went hungry. He asked for nothing in return. No, that's not true. He never stopped pleading with me to see you. Until the day he died, your father never gave up hoping I would see you again. I couldn't, Edwin; I was too scared. Despite what your father said, I knew that if you saw me you would have no choice but to hate me.

It's your birthday today, Edwin. You're no longer a child but a grown man. I've missed your life: you have gone from being a seven-year-old to being an adult and I know nothing about you

– nothing but the snippets your father told me. Oh, Edwin . . . what have I done?

You used to sit on my knee as I played the piano. Do you remember that? When you were young, you used to rest your small hands on the backs of mine as I played. We played together – 'Clair de Lune', the Moonlight Sonata – you liked those slow, sad pieces best of all. I recall those afternoons when we used to play – your hands on mine as if we were joined together. If only we could have stayed like that forever, Edwin.

The last time your father visited he brought me an envelope. Inside, he told me, was a photograph of you. He didn't make me open it – he simply put it on my table as he left. He died shortly after that visit. I carry that envelope around with me but I have never opened it. I lack the courage to do so. I know you are inside but I don't know if I can bear to see you again. The first time I laid eyes on you, Edwin, I thought you were the most beautiful child in the world. You were perfect, yet I couldn't come to terms with the fact that you were mine, that you came from me. I felt as if you were a gift, that you had been given to me and I was embarrassed by the giver's generosity . . . I didn't feel connected to you. I was never what people call maternal. I've never managed to be a good mother.

Time passes slowly now. Thomas has been dead many years and not a day passes when I don't ache from the emptiness I feel. I miss him so much, Edwin. I loved him so completely. I never stopped being 'in love' with him. But, Edwin, I grieve for you too.

ONE

Edwin clutched the daffodils to him, their cellophane wrapping crushed in his hand. He felt the need to hold on to something but, looking around, he could see nothing strong enough to support his weight. A few residents of the home passed by, their hands gripped around the bars of Zimmer frames or the metal rail that ran the length of the corridor, all the way from the foyer, where he stood, to the room where his mother was waiting. Neither would do. He imagined that if he was to reach out for the rail his hand, like that of a ghost, would pass right through the metal and he would lose his balance and fall on his face.

Matilda had gone ahead with Beth. The last he had seen of her was a brief smile as she followed Beth down the corridor. He had been told to wait. Beth was to get her mother – their mother – settled and then come back for him.

'She's looking forward to seeing you,' Beth had reassured him, her expression belying the upbeat tone of her voice. 'She doesn't get many visitors.'

As the words left Beth's mouth Edwin understood that, like him, she was nervous. She hadn't meant to say that. Catching herself, she quickly added, 'She gets confused, she's old and

doesn't always understand what's . . . she gets very confused . . .'
Beth had not finished the sentence. She had already warned
Edwin that Jess was an elderly woman. That she tended to repeat
herself, ask the same question over and over again – that type
of thing. She didn't have Alzheimer's but she was suffering from
some kind of dementia. She was usually pretty good around Beth
and the nurses, because their faces were familiar, but she might
not respond so well to Edwin. There was a chance she might not
recognise him after all these years. It was also possible she might
not know who he was. She might have forgotten she had a son.
He should just take things slowly. It would be fine. Beth would
be there. It would be fine.

A nurse approached, touched him lightly on the sleeve and
said, 'Why don't you go down now? Beth says it's all right.'
Hearing her voice, Edwin jumped, his legs all but giving way. He
tried to smile at the nurse but his lips trembled and it was all he
could do to nod. He glanced around him, noted that the lights
were all turned on, even though it was mid-afternoon and the
sun was pouring in through the double doors behind him.

Slowly, he took a step and then stopped, gasping for breath.
The nurse, who was beside him, took him by the elbow but he
waved her away. 'I'm all right,' he whispered, his voice hoarse.
'I'll be there in a minute.' He saw the nurse smile and step back.
He caught her eye and said, 'I'm sorry. For some reason I feel a
bit jittery. I'll be fine in a minute.'

Glancing down to his hands, he registered that the bunch
of daffodils was shaking. He tried to still the flowers by taking
the bouquet in both hands but they continued to shudder. He
smoothed the wrapper around them, running one hand over
the cellophane as if trying to smooth a sheet, but the crinkles

seemed imprinted – there was no way he could straighten them. The nurse was still beside him and he tried to smile once more. 'I haven't seen my mother since I was seven – fifty-five years ago.' He nodded his head several times as if needing to confirm what he had said in order to make it true, then, suddenly self-conscious, he shrugged, caught himself shrugging and shrugged again. 'Sorry.'

A figure appeared at the end of the corridor. It was Beth. She raised her hand to beckon him forward but as she looked at him, she hesitated, raising her hand to her face instead, covering her mouth with her palm. She stood like that for several seconds, then Edwin saw her shoulders give way and shudder and he looked down, helpless.

'Matilda is in there,' he murmured. 'She'll be wondering what's going on.' He took a step forward, and another, but his vision began to blur. Tears filled his eyes and he wiped his eyes with the back of his hand. Patting his pockets, he realised he had come out without a handkerchief. A memory came back to him: a folded plain white handkerchief his mother passed to him on the day she left. 'Take this,' she had murmured as she straightened his shirt before he jumped into the truck next to Samuel. 'You'll need it later.'

'I used to wait for you to come back,' Edwin whispered as he reached the door at the end of the corridor. It was his mother's room. Her nameplate was attached by four screws to the door. Looking at her name, he ran his fingers over the letters like a blind man reading Braille. He stopped midway through her surname; she had the same name as him – not her maiden name or Thomas's name but his father's name, Edwin's name. She had kept the name. Placing one palm on the door, he took the handle with the other and pushed gently. The door caught on the carpet pile, making a soft shush as it dragged across the floor. He glanced down and edged soundlessly inside.

ACKNOWLEDGEMENTS

Parts of this novel are set in the TB sanatorium at Waipiata in Central Otago. Although the sanatorium existed and the buildings are still in use today, I have taken certain liberties in describing the place and the events that took place there. A pamphlet describing the establishment of the sanatorium, entitled *Waipiata Sanatorium: A Brief History of a Successful Institution*, published in 1928, makes fascinating reading. It is available in the Dunedin Public Library.

I would like to thank Kate Thompson and Lynne Knapp at the University of Otago Medical Library for allowing me access to several documents relating to the sanatorium, most notably W. E. Chisholm's 'Waipiata Sanatorium', a thesis written during the summer of 1948–49. I would also like to thank Debbie Dunsford for her helpful suggestions as I began to research the history of tuberculosis in this country.

I would like to thank Nadine Newton for her descriptions of Banana, and I would also like to acknowledge the support of Arts Tasmania and the Tasmanian Writers' Centre through its Island of Residencies Program.

There are several other people I would especially like to

thank: my husband, Alexander McLellan, for his support and understanding; Sue Wootton and Bill Manhire for reading and commenting on parts of my manuscript; and Dr Garry Nixon for answering my many medical questions. I am very grateful for their help and encouragement.

I would also like to thank Geoff Walker and Rebecca Lal at Penguin and Rachel Scott for their ongoing support.

To all of these people I am deeply indebted.